Magnifico

Magnifico

VICTORIA MILES

Fitzhenry & Whiteside

Published in Canada by Fitzhenry & Whiteside, 195 Allstate Parkway, Markham, Ontario L3R 4T8

Published in the United States by Fitzhenry & Whiteside, 311 Washington Street, Brighton, Massachusetts 02135

www.fitzhenry.ca   godwit@fitzhenry.ca

Library and Archives Canada Cataloguing in Publication

Miles, Victoria, 1966-
   Magnifico / Victoria Miles.

ISBN 1-55041-960-9
   I. Title.
PS8576.I3235M33 2006   jC813'.54   C2005-907257-1

U.S. Publisher Cataloging-in-Publication Data (Library of Congress Standards)

Miles, Victoria, 1966–
   Magnifico / Victoria Miles.
[256] p.: cm.
Summary: Mariangela longs to play the piano, but her Italian immigrant family arranges for accordion lessons instead, and she is mortified when her reluctant struggle to make the bulky old instrument sing appears doomed to failure.
ISBN 1-55041-960-9

1. Musicians—Fiction. 2. Immigrants—Fiction. 3. Accordion—Fiction. I. Title.
[Fic] dc22   PZ7.M5537Ma   2006

Fitzhenry & Whiteside acknowledges with thanks the Canada Council for the Arts, and the Ontario Arts Council for their support of our publishing program. We acknowledge the financial support of the Government of Canada through the Book Publishing Industry Development Program (BPIDP) for our publishing activities.

 Canada Council   Conseil des Arts
for the Arts   du Canada

Design by Fortunato Design Inc.
Cover image by Tara Anderson

Printed in Canada

10 9 8 7 6 5 4 3 2 1

For Grandad and Nana,
who bought the Hohner,
"because there was no money
for a piano"
and for my mother, Joan,
who learned to play it

CHAPTER 1
The White Camroni

January, 1939

IT WAS THERE—the suitcase—on the carpet, in the middle of the living room. It was the first Tuesday after Christmas break, when Sonia and I got home from school. At first I thought we had a visitor. There was a chicken roasting in the oven and sauce on the stove, so it smelled like company was coming. Exciting for us, since Mamma hardly ever let anyone but family past our front door. Or maybe we had a new boarder for the basement. But I was wrong. Something very different had come to stay.

We heard voices from the kitchen, murmurs in Italian, as we circled the curious case. It was hard-shelled, like an upholstered turtle wearing a pattern of beige and black houndstooth—but smart for a piece of luggage.

The suitcase was not a *suit case*, a case for suits. While the side that had greeted us was smooth and flat, its opposite was bent and sloped deliberately at the center. Was it protecting the keys of a typewriter? Sonia thought so. What else could it be?

Nothing else could be assumed without opening it. In the kitchen, Mamma and Nonna sat at the table. Two cups of *caffè* and a plate of small, round cookies were between them. Our little sister Emelina made growling noises down on the floor. She pushed Billydog, the stuffed lamb Mamma had made her for Christmas, up one of Nonna's legs. It was our absolutely ordinary after-school scene. No salesman. No new boarder—just Nonna coming by, as she did nearly every day. She took our faces in hands softened with olive oil and kissed us hello on both cheeks. Then Sonia asked whose case it was, in the living room. Mamma didn't say anything. She went calmly to the icebox for the milk, and then she busied herself taking down glasses from the cupboard for us.

"The case," answered Nonna, in Italian, "and what's inside, they belong to Mariangela."

My stomach first leaped, then lurched. A gift? But the case was rough at the edges, not new. It couldn't be a present. Christmas was almost a month behind us; my birthday wasn't till June. I had been asking for a piano. Cousin Gigi had a piano. And this year, my father just laughed on Christmas morning. "A piano? Who has money for a piano?" Sonia, who was nine, and Emelina, who was three, got toys. But I was eleven—too old for toys, too young for silk stockings, said Papa. There might have been books, had my parents known how to choose them. I had asked for *The Wizard of Oz*, but my mother did the shopping, and she never went into bookshops.

So my eleventh, my Christmas of 1938, was

all dull brown—woolen stockings, underwear, and two new dresses Mamma had made. Because I had my doubts about my chances for a piano, I'd asked for roller skates, which only cost a couple of dollars. I didn't get those, either.

Too bad for you, Mariangela.

I had been asking for the piano since I was eight. Although I had secretly given up, I asked again anyway, just to make the point. I had discovered the Principle of the Thing. My piano was no whim. I was meant to play piano. I knew it. I dreamt it.

I envied Cousin Gigi's upright piano to the point of confession. To Father Paul at Sacred Heart, I confessed to envy, once. But as the envy did not go away after my dutiful Hail Marys, I did not tell him again.

"Come on, Mariangela, I show-a you some-atin," said Nonna, this time in her broken English, as she led the way back into the living room. Emelina and Sonia stayed close to the cookies. Mamma, still calm and silent, followed us to the doorway. She leaned against the door-frame and crossed her arms. Nothing on her face hinted whether the case held good or bad. Maybe she didn't know.

"Open it," said Nonna, standing over the case. Her eyes were excited and shining. I knelt down, laid the heavy case on its flat side, and pressed the locks sideways. They snapped open hard against my thumbs. I bounced back, a little surprised by the petty pain they struck.

"Go on now, lift the lid," Nonna coaxed. Her voice came out in a happy kind of anxiousness that said, *Come with me on this; don't disappoint me.*

I did as she said, nervous now because I had a good idea of what the case really contained. The inside was lined in crumpled blue velvet. A scrap of navy blue velvet covered the contents—the gift I had always dreaded—for one last safe moment.

I remembered remarks slipped by Uncle Tony about "my some-a day inheritance," always accompanied by Mamma's sister, Zia Letizia's, sympathetic silence. They let on what I always knew—my musical *destino* (destiny) would come for me one day. I sat still with disappointment as my piano dream ebbed away behind me…down the hall and out the front door.

Nonna bent down and, with a little flourish and a sigh, whisked the blue cloth away.

And there it was—the accordion. Ivory-colored panels decorated with a flower, cutouts of swirls and rhinestones, and in the center, a musical lyre. Both sides of the accordion were carved to look like lightning bolts. And running down the grille was the name "Camroni," spelled out in glittering rhinestones.

I knew it by its family story. It was my Nonno's accordion. Nonno, who died in Italy before I was born. Nonna had brought two suitcases with her when she came to Canada, and the accordion was in one of them. It had sat in the back of her closet, at Uncle Tony and Zia Letizia's house. And it hadn't left its case since Nonno died.

"But Nonna, what did you bring for meeeeeee?" Sonia squealed as she squeezed past Mamma. And as Sonia reached out to touch the accordion, Nonna gently swatted back her cookie-crumbed hand.

"Dis notta toy. You keepa dis-a clean, Mariangela. Polish it some-a da time," said Nonna firmly.

"And you?" she said to my sister. "You no touch." She squeezed Sonia's fingers and kissed them, but the tone of her voice was firm. "You see?" she said, pointing to the ivory keys. "No stain from your Nonno's fingers. Notta mark. All *perfetto*, juss-a like new."

I couldn't say anything. I looked more closely. The black and white keys were mother-of-pearl beautiful. I counted them: forty-one.

My thought then was small and envious.

Cousin Gigi's piano had a lot more keys. I didn't know how many, just more. It was also the rows of tiny black buttons that made me nervous about the accordion; there were too many to count—at least a hundred. At least. A few of the buttons held tiny rhinestones. I reached out and pressed one. Nothing. I pressed another. Nothing again. I pushed down a whole bunch together—still no sound. I touched a key down. That too, was note-less.

"Ah, but-ta you have to make it breathe," said Nonna. She squatted down and, with a grunt, lifted out the accordion and set it on the coffee table. She held out the straps and waved her hand for me to come closer. I bent down and awkwardly put my arms through the straps. When I stood back, I almost fell over from the weight of it. It felt like a barrel had been bound to my chest—or a tree trunk. It was heavier than Emelina, than anything I'd ever been made to carry.

Mamma was behind me, her hand on my shoulder. She led me backward to the sofa. The accordion knocked my knees. Nonna couldn't stop now. She unsnapped two small bands of leather, and the bellows slowly fell open to my left. I caught them and squeezed the box closed.

"Pull-a dem out, and press-a da key," said Nonna. I did, and out came a startling note. Cheerful, bright-sounding, it made Nonna's face flush. She fanned herself with one hand over her heart. "Push now, and press a button."

I pushed, fumbled for a button, and *zaaaaaaaaaaaahhh*—a bold chord came through. Like a harmonica, only louder, richer. I pushed harder, and the bellows sealed back against each other and cut the chord off.

"Look at me! Look at me!" Emelina crowed. She was sitting in the accordion case and trying to close the lid over her head. Mamma held the lid up and pulled her out; Emelina giggled. I tried

15

another key and pulled the bellows, then a few more. The notes didn't match. It was awful, and the sound died on me as soon as I forgot to pull.

Emelina slapped her hands against her ears. "I'm running away!" she shouted, and tore into the kitchen.

Sonia was already there, probably pilfering candy from Nonna's handbag, which she did openly and routinely every time Nonna visited. I heard Emelina squeal, "*Torrone!* Yay!" *Torrone* was my favorite; usually Nonna only bought it at Christmas. But I was stuck out in the living room, anchored to the sofa by the white Camroni.

Too bad for you, Mariangela!

Listlessly, I pulled the bellows again, and tapped a few more keys.

Gradually, Nonna's expression changed. I knew the notes I played made no sense. But still, I could see in her face that her memories had drawn her across land and sea to Italy. I knew that faraway look; Mamma got it too, sometimes.

"Your grandfather, this-a his riches," Nonna said. "He had-da clothes and music-a—that's-a all. The music-a, Mariangela, she in that case a long-a, long-a time. You to let-ta her out. I'm old, and I need-a to hear her again."

I know I should have. But I couldn't bring myself to say yes.

I *would* do it. I would bring it all back for her. I looked down at all those impossible buttons and keys. Couldn't she see how hopeless it was? The straps were cutting into my shoulders. I pushed myself up, one hand on an armrest, the way pregnant Mamma used to, when she was heavy with Emelina. I tried first to shrug out of the straps, but I didn't trust my arms to take the weight. So I did the only thing I could think of; I knelt down on the floor and squirmed free— wriggled out backward like a dumpy duck. I was careful. I didn't want to play it, but I didn't want to break it, either.

At least not yet.

CHAPTER 2
Some Secret Thing

MY MOTHER HAD LIVED in Canada for thirteen years. And in all that time she never unpacked her suitcase. It wasn't like she wore the same dress every day, but we all knew that she kept a case packed under her bed. It was Sonia who found it the summer before the accordion arrived, and she showed it to me.

We were fascinated. There were clothes we'd never seen Mamma wear—stockings, a pair of shoes, a bracelet, two sweaters, and an old coat. A tiny bottle—half-full of amber-colored perfume—which was sticky-brown at the neck, where it had leaked. Even a compact and mirror, and a small change purse filled with Italian coins. And tucked inside a satin-covered pocket was a crinkled envelope with a single crescent of soft, blonde baby hair. It looked like one of Emelina's curls.

Mamma hadn't cut her hair since arriving in Canada. Her coloring was very different from Sonia's and mine. Mamma was fair, with blue eyes and long blonde hair, which she wore every day divided into two thick braids, pinned around her head like a coronet. And she was slim as spaghetti, except for her face, which was round, pale, and pretty. And she was as tall as Father, taller in heels.

I was proud of Mamma's beauty. We all were. And no mother in the East End had hair like Mamma's. Most wore theirs cut and rolled under at the chin, parted on one side and neatly waved. It was as if my mother never noticed the style. Sometimes on Saturday mornings, we would walk by Vanelli's Barbershop on our way downtown. Mr. Vanelli would call out, "Signora Benetti! How much for your hair? I buy, any day! Any day! You jus' say!"

Mamma just smiled at Mr. Vanelli and shooed us along. On the street, even the Italians spoke English. Except for my mother—she had so little English that, out-of-doors, she hardly spoke at all. She shopped in the Italian grocery stores, and if a trip to another store was unavoidable, she took us with her to translate.

The first time we heard Mr. Vanelli, Sonia and I thought he had to be joking, but Mamma said no, barbers bought hair all the time, then sold it again to wigmakers.

"So you sell your hair, so that someone else will wear it?"

"Yes," said Mamma. "Only I'm not selling."

I was relieved. It was a shame I hadn't any of Mamma's beauty myself. I had olive skin; short, wonky brown hair that curled up on one side and under on the other; a space between my front teeth; wide, flat feet; and knees that faced each other. Worst of all were my eyebrows—two thick black swatches above eyes as round as a cow's. Chubby Sonia was the prettier version of me, with everything in proportion—her teeth tight and small, her eyes not quite so large, and her brows thin and arching, just like her feet. Emelina was like Mamma in miniature, only her blonde hair curled like Shirley Temple's. Envy of my three-year-old sister, just for being beautiful, once cost me three Hail Marys at confession.

Going back to Italy was something Mamma never talked to us about. But we knew she thought about it. We could see her memories take her there sometimes.

Lugging the accordion up the stairs made me think of Mamma's suitcase. On each step, I grunted like Quasimodo and yanked the case up after me.

"Leave it for your father to do!" Mamma yelled from the landing.

We yelled a lot in our house. Yelling was okay, so long as you closed the windows. But I didn't want to wait for Papa. I wanted to get the accordion into my closet, and out of my sight, before he came home. Maybe he didn't have to know.

Nobody in our family ever went anywhere. That's what made Mamma's suitcase so mysterious. My parents had made their one great *viaggio* (voyage), and then they never traveled again.

One day, months after the suitcase discovery, Sonia was in our parents' room again. She'd pulled out Mamma's case and was going through it, which had become one of her favorite things to do. It was better even than searching through Nonna's purse. She was sure there was something else hidden in that case— some secret thing. She didn't ask permission, but Sonia was so obvious about everything she did that it was always only a matter of time until she got caught.

It was Emelina who spilled the beans. I was with Mamma in the sewing room at that moment. I was cutting pieces for a little coat for Billydog. Mamma was hemming a dress. Emelina came into the room singing, "Sonia's in da sooootcase," and tugged on Mamma's skirt.

Straightaway, Mamma took the pin out of her mouth. "Whose suitcase?" she asked.

"Da sooootcase under da Mamma bed," said Emelina.

Mamma stuck the pin into the little felt tomato she wore around her wrist, and rushed out of the room.

We found Sonia kneeling in front of the open suitcase, dabbing on a little of the musty perfume. Sonia was right on the mark.

"Mamma, why do you have a suitcase full of stuff under your bed?"

Sonia never understood the point of keeping a secret. She had a way of asking questions so right-between-the-eyes that you found yourself answering before you could even think that it wasn't any of her business—and how was it she knew enough to ask, in the first place? She was especially good at being direct with adults, including our parents. Nobody ever expected it from a nine-year-old. Grown-ups would answer first, and then looked stunned afterward by whatever truth they'd confessed.

Mamma took the compact out of Sonia's hand and tidied the clothes before closing the case and sliding it back under the bed. She looked at all of us first, then her gaze traveled across the room, out the window, over the rooftop of the house across from ours and away.

Lucky Sonia! Mamma wasn't angry. She was off to her faraway place.

"In case we ever go back," said Mamma plainly, "I want to be ready."

After that, the mystique of Mamma's suitcase was lost for all three of us. But we still looked under the bed, every once in a while, to see if it was still there; and we tugged at it to check the weight, to see if she'd unpacked it yet.

She never did.

CHAPTER 3
Ciribiribin

THE NIGHT THE ACCORDION CAME, Mamma set an extra place on the white lace tablecloth that covered our round kitchen table. We were having a roast chicken, ziti in tomato sauce, bread and vegetables, and chicken with rice soup to start. In the icebox was a creamy cassata cake for dessert. Except for the cake—we only had cassata for birthdays—the rest of dinner was not really special food, unless you put it all together. Papa swapped vegetables from our garden for homemade red wine from our neighbors. I poured little glasses for everybody except Emelina. She got milk. Sonia liked the wine; it turned her face red, and she got giggly. Mamma talked a lot about cutting her off— it interfered with her homework. Wine tasted sour to me; I always left mine for Papa to drink.

Then I went out to the parlor, where Sonia and Emelina were playing. Emelina had her new store-bought Christmas doll, Baby Bubbles, riding on top of Hippo-the-Potamus, which Mamma had made for Sonia when she was a baby. Mamma was a beautiful seamstress; she made most of our clothes, and she sewed for people in the neighborhood. Sometimes she took orders from Mr. Zucchi for the department stores.

Hippo-the-Potamus was an experiment that Mamma had made with scraps. I think Mamma might have meant him to be an elephant, but he was purple and his trunk was too short. He looked more like an eggplant with eyes. When Sonia started talking, she just insisted his name was Hippo-the-Potamus. It stuck.

Waiting for dinner, Sonia had her scrapbook out. She was pasting in her Christmas cards, and she had a big stack to get through. Sonia was popular. She was quick at games like dodge ball and kick the can, and light as a flea when she jumped rope. And she was smart; everyone said so. She spoke a little bit of Japanese—lots of kids at Strathcona School were Japanese—as well as English, Italian, and even some Greek. She was the first to talk to new kids at school, and if they didn't share a language, she'd just use her hands more. I often saw her in the schoolyard at recess, waving her hands wildly and laughing—mimicking teachers or trying to explain how to play baseball.

We heard Papa's footsteps coming up to the back door, and raced into the kitchen.

"Mariangela got an accordion!" Sonia burst out as Papa opened the door.

"Yah! It's really bad!" cried Emelina.

My father was pleased. Not surprised. Pleased. Definitely my parents were in cahoots on this. He took off his coat, unwound his scarf, and gave us all a kiss: Mamma first, then Sonia, Emelina, and me. He scooped Emelina up and sat her on his shoulders. Crouching down, so she wouldn't knock her head in the doorway, he mock-ordered her in a voice so deep that it made the windows waver.

"Onward! Lead on to the magnificent accordion!" Emelina squealed with delight, tugged on his graying hair, and pointed upstairs.

"Heigh ho!" said Papa, charging out to the hall and up the stairs.

I dragged myself behind them as if I were towing an anchor. Papa had the Camroni out on my bed when I got to the door.

"Ah, now that's a beautiful instrument, Mariangela," he said, sweeping the cloth over the keys. "Aren't you a lucky girl?"

I moved my cheeks, deliberately, to make my unluckiest smile.

Papa was thick around his middle. His belly had begun to poke out over his belt, and Mamma was always warning him, as she contentedly piled his plate with seconds, that he would have to be careful or he'd soon "go to fat." He had soft jowls, which were beginning to draw his cheeks down, and two deep creases encircling his mouth—made deeper by his firm opinion that *un giorno sensa sorrisi è un giorno sprecato* (a day without laughter is a day wasted). He was as dark as Mamma was fair—all year round.

He sat down heavily on my bed. He weighed the corner under him so deeply that it pulled the covers, and I would have to remake it when he got up. He pressed a key on the accordion.

"No, no, Papa!" Sonia tsked, sucking air through her teeth and doing her best Nonna impersonation. "You have to make it breeeeathe!"

Papa picked up the accordion, and was about to try it on, when the front doorbell rang. Emelina froze with excitement and Sonia bolted out of the room. She loved to answer the door first. For Sonia, anything new was welcome— the stranger the better. I was more like Mamma. When I was small, and it was just me and

Mamma in the house, I learned that front door-
bells announced people to be shy of, people she
might not understand. She would hang back
from answering, if she could, and I would hide
behind her skirt.

This time, though, Mamma beat her to it.
This ring she was ready for and pleased to
answer. Her apron was gone and she smoothed
her hair. Then, just before Sonia could make a
grab for the knob, Mamma reached to open the
door.

There, on our front porch, stood a young
man we all recognized but didn't know. He had
thick, black hair, close cropped and glossy. His
skin was the warm color of brick and his dark
eyes were friendly. He was a little shorter than
my father and, perhaps, too thin—for sure
Mamma would say so at the table. Pretty much
everyone looked as lean as a stalk of asparagus
when they stood next to Papa. Papa was more
like a potato.

The young man's name was Gioseff DeMarco. We saw him around the neighborhood now and again because he painted signs for shops and businesses. He even painted the little block of wood Mamma had in the window of our house: Carmella Benetti, Dressmaking, Inquire Saturdays. It had to be Saturdays because Papa was home to translate. I remember the day the sign was put up. When Papa saw it, he was mad about the Saturday thing. He wanted to paint over it.

"You've got to learn English, Carmella!" he yelled. "How are you going to learn if I have to talk for you?" But Mamma insisted it was either that, or she wouldn't sew. No sewing, no extra money. Saturdays stuck.

Gioseff looked a little nervous, and then I realized we were all gawking at him.

"Come in, come in! Welcome!" boomed my father with his usual enthusiasm. Gioseff squeezed into the crowded hallway. Papa put out his hand and Gioseff shook it, keeping his left hand in his coat pocket.

All through dinner, Emelina and Sonia stared silently across the table at Gioseff. Not because they longed for a big brother (they did) and had me instead (did they think God had finally answered their prayers?), but because of his left hand. Where there should have been a baby and a ring finger, there were only two short stumps. I sat on Gioseff's left side, making a thorough study difficult, but I noticed that the skin was gathered to the center of each stump, and drawn neatly inward, like the navel of an orange.

Gioseff didn't seem self-conscious about his hand. He didn't mind the blank stares of Emelina and Sonia, their faces greasy from chicken drumsticks—the only part they would eat. Lucky thing God gave a chicken two legs, so my sisters could eat without bickering.

Because Sonia acted as if she'd been struck dumb by lightning, it fell to Papa to drill Gioseff.

At first I thought he might be here to rent our basement suite. But Gioseff, it turned out, played the accordion. He'd been playing for twenty years or more. He must've told Mamma when he painted her sign.

"Piano accordion?" asked my father, turning serious for a brief moment.

"Yes, sir. That, and concertina. I know a little harmonica, too."

Harmonica. Now that could be fun. The accordion was like having a bear in the bedroom. But a harmonica, that might be okay. A couple of boys at school had them.

"No harmonica," said Papa, polite but firm, looking at me. He must've seen me drift off. I had my mother's "traveling" habit, and just like her, it showed on my face. "It's not for girls."

"How much would you charge to give lessons?"—this from Mamma, who was unfailingly careful with money.

"A dollar an hour," said Gioseff.

A dollar an hour. One whole dollar every week. Here was hope! The deal breaker! My parents would never part with a whole dollar every Saturday.

I glanced furtively at Mamma, and what I saw made my heart sink. She was smiling at Gioseff, as if a dollar an hour were a bargain at twice the price.

"Can you come to the house? Teach her here?" asked Papa.

Gioseff said, "Sure, no problem."

Papa nodded with satisfaction. Whether he knew it or not, Gioseff had made his way to the final condition.

"Can you play 'Ciribiribin'?" asked Papa.

"Yes, sir."

Papa pushed his chair back, rose from the table and headed upstairs. He came down again with the accordion, and wordlessly handed it to Gioseff.

"'Ciribiribin,'" announced Gioseff formally,

as he slid easily into the instrument and unsnapped the bellows.

"Ciribiribin" was Papa's favorite song—about a pretty girl with a pretty mouth, pretty nose, pretty eyes. He'd sing it to Mamma, and to the three of us when we were small. A bad performance of "Ciribiribin" and Gioseff could kiss his dollar-a-week good-bye. I crossed my fingers under the table.

With his head bowed toward the keyboard and his eyes closed, he played it perfectly. Bright, light, and cheery—a music-box melody for which a tiny doll should pirouette. Under the table I could hear my father's foot tapping along with the tune. Gioseff's fingers were fast on the keys and buttons. Especially on the left-side buttons, where he only had the two. They moved too fast to follow. I think my jaw must've dropped a little because when he finished, he looked at me and said, "Don't worry, Mariangela. You don't have to learn that till the second lesson!"

Papa thought that was funny, so he laughed, which made Sonia and Emelina laugh, and Mamma smile—not at the joke she didn't understand, but at the mirth around the table.

Too bad for you again, Mariangela.

So, as my mother cut the cake and passed slices round the table, my musical *destino* was bandied back and forth a little longer. By the time my father pushed his chair back and tipped his glass toward Gioṣeff, they had the details of my accordion lessons pinned down tightly—like a tightly-pegged tent, against my opposing wind.

CHAPTER 4

Scrapbook English

MY FATHER LEARNED HIS ENGLISH from the newspaper. He spoke perfect *Vancouver Sun* with only a trace of an accent. He had come to Canada before my mother, and after he had found work, he sent for her. She came with Nonna, and they were reunited with Uncle Tony and Aunt Letizia, who by then had baby Gigi.

Lately, Papa had become very serious when he sat down to read the paper. The headlines were always about news from Europe. The papers reported daily on the threat of war, and on the different presidents and prime ministers who were desperately trying to steer Hitler and Mussolini back toward peace. It seemed that the news became more hopeless, the possibility of peace more distant, every time Papa picked up the paper. At the same time, war I couldn't imagine. I would listen to Papa grumble about Hitler and Il Duce, but for me, the stories in the newspaper were like shouts coming from men miles away—barely in sight. You could see their lips moving, but you were not close enough to understand what they were saying.

When Papa finished with a section, he would hand it down to Sonia, who sat on the floor with a bottle of LePage's glue, scissors, and her giant scrapbook. I liked the paper, too—especially the serial stories, "Ripley's Believe it or Not," "Little Annie Rooney," and "Roy Powers King's Scout" comics. And I especially liked Annie Rooney. People were always talking "the blarney" to her, and she had the neatest expressions. If something was really wonderful, she'd say, "Gloryosky, that's grand!"

The "Imagine My Embarrassment" stories were good, too. One man wrote in about how he'd knocked over all the pies at a Sunday picnic;

a woman said she'd run out of her house to join the neighbors in shooing a bear away, to realize a moment later she was only wearing a slip. And there was the lady whose bottle of homemade wine exploded on a streetcar. The stories were mostly funny, and the paper paid a dollar for every one they printed.

But my favorite section of the paper was the Lucky Badge contest. I had my own Lucky Badge number: 207303. I'd check the paper every day to see if the numbers matched. A match won you two free tickets to a double feature at the Orpheum Theater. We didn't get pocket money, but I had faith in the Lucky Badge contest. I'd been following it for two years, and every day I felt like I was due. Sonia tried to get me to promise to take her to the pictures if I won, but I was already torn between taking Esther or Dot—my two best friends.

Sonia was a fiend for all things royal. She would clip and paste anything from the newspaper about the princesses, Elizabeth and Margaret, King George, and Queen Elizabeth. She had eyebrows just like me: dark and thick, they reached out to the fringes of her waved black hair. Only on her, they were beautiful. The queen's eyebrows gave me hope.

Pasted around the edges of Sonia's royal clippings were Christmas and birthday cards, Valentines, labels from her favorite candy bars (one whole page was devoted to Cadbury's, another to Sweet Marie), her saint cards from Sunday school, and Italian postage stamps that were trimmed from envelopes addressed to Mamma.

The night after Gioseff's visit, Sonia began a new page in her scrapbook. Mamma took Emelina up, to tuck in bed, and Papa settled down, in his chair in the living room, with the evening paper. Sonia kneeled beside him, on the floor, and waited patiently for the first page. When Papa handed down the front page of *The*

Vancouver Sun, she squealed with delight over the headline: "The King and Queen Here May 29; Will Proceed to Victoria on Same Day."

"Listen to this," Sonia said. "'Society circles are agog speculating on the possibility of being presented to their Majesties.' Oh! Can you imagine being presented to the king and queen?" Sonia stood up and made a deep curtsey, her left foot behind her right—the proper way that the newspaper had stressed. "Pleased to meet you, your Majesty. I am *agog*, your Majesty," she said, with her hand over her heart. It sounded like play-acting, but behind the curtain of Sonia's performance, I recognized the sound of a wild idea beginning in her soul.

Maybe Papa sensed it, too. He knew to be wary of just how far Sonia could take a thought.

"Now Sonia, you're not society. You're a subject," he said to her seriously.

"But it says here the quints will get to meet them. And they're subjects! We're all subjects!"

Sonia said impatiently, as if Papa were a dimwit.

"Well, yes, but they're the Dionne Quintuplets. Everyone in the world has heard of them. Even the king and queen have never seen five identical twins. They are very interesting little girls."

"I'm a very interesting little girl!" Papa was not going to win this one.

"Yes, you are, and it's a shame the king and queen won't get to meet you, or your very interesting sisters. You know thousands of people will be out to see the king and queen. We'll be in a crowd of many. You can't expect them to see, with all those people, how special you are."

Sonia shrugged, grumbled something about how you had to be a triplet or a quad or a quint to get any attention in this world. And then, just like that, the idea vanished from her eyes without even a hurt look at Papa. Sonia was easy about letting things go. But I was like Mamma; I stewed like tomatoes in a hot oven. I'd go over a thing and over a thing, even when every last shred of hope was gone. Surely, if I groped around in the dark long enough, a new idea would come to save me from the cursed Camroni.

An advertisement on one of the pages Sonia had discarded for her scrapbook caught my eye. At Lewis Piano House, you could buy a piano for a dollar down and a dollar a week! I grabbed the scissors, cut out the ad, and slipped it onto Papa's armrest.

"Look, Papa! A dollar a week for a piano. It's a special price! You could save the money from Gioseff, and we could have a piano instead!"

"And who would teach you the piano?" asked my father, without looking up from his page.

"Me! I could learn. I could teach myself."

"You can't teach yourself the piano."

"Maybe Gigi could teach me."

Papa sighed and put down his paper. "Mariangela, you already have an instrument—

an orchestra unto itself. The money for accordion lessons is from your Nonna. It's not for a piano. I tell you what—you see how you do with the accordion, then we'll talk about the piano."

My parents were masters of the easy out: the perfect foil. Mamma could knot a loophole so tight, even a hatpin couldn't get through. It was what Papa called "being reasonable." They had to know I was never going to learn the crummy accordion, so that meant I had no chance at a piano. I took the advertisement back, crumpled it in my hand, and shoved it dejectedly into my skirt pocket. I found the Family Features and scanned the columns for the day's Lucky Badge winner.

207304. What? Not 207303? How crummy can you get, to miss it by one. What kind of luck is that?

I studied that number hard. Somebody else was going to see *The Shining Hour* with Joan Crawford (who also had thick eyebrows, but always looked kind of hysterical-crazy) and *Spring Madness* with Maureen O'Sullivan. It wasn't going to be me. How could I miss it by one?

Too bad for you, Mariangela.

Thass-a jus' yo kind-a luck.

CHAPTER 5

What Dot and Esther Said

OUR HOUSE WAS ONLY A COUPLE of blocks from school. We were at the end of a long row of tall houses, all with the same steeply peaked roofs, and we faced the snow-capped North Shore mountains, which looked like sentries on guard in the middle of the city.

We lived so close to school that, from my house, we could all make it without pulling up our stockings once. This was something Esther noticed first, and it became her way of measuring distance forever after. How far to Woolworth's downtown department store? You'd have to pull up your stockings a dozen times on the way. But to the Montreal Bakery, where Mamma sent us for bread, or Mr. Stefani's store, where we bought milk, it was only one pull-up—two, if we dawdled. So it usually took two pull-ups. Of all of us, Esther had the farthest to walk. In winter, on the way to Dot's house and then on to my house, she had to wear boy's trousers under her dresses, to keep her legs warm.

Dot's father was a logger. He wasn't around much, but Dot had nice store-bought clothes, and she got pocket money for her chores. Dot didn't have brothers or sisters, so once she'd taken me to see a Charlie Chan show at the Princess. Another time, she treated Esther.

Esther's parents had a wagon, and a little pony they kept in a shed behind their house. While Esther was in school, they collected the junk that people threw into the alleys. They traded it or sold it, and that was how they got by. Esther was the oldest kid in her family, but she still wore hand-me-downs—she just never knew exactly who'd handed them down. I sometimes felt sorry for Esther. Her house was stuffed with dusty junk and we could never play there. And nobody, at the Princess, or the Bijou Star, or the Maple Leaf Theater, would let her trade something from off her Daddy's wagon for a ticket.

Mamma liked Dot. If she stayed after school for supper, she always said, "*Per favore*" and "*Grazie*" to Mamma, even though her family was from Liverpool, England. Dot wasn't phony. She really liked eating at our house—she always said her mother would never cook spaghetti, no matter how much she begged. Her mother made food with strange names that I gave up trying to explain to Mamma: toad-in-the-hole, pigs-in-blankets, bubble-and-squeak...

Mamma would go around the table and fill our plates with seconds; and, if I picked at mine, she'd ask why I couldn't be more like Dot. Dot was a "good eater." In our house, that was high praise. They liked Esther too, but my parents were especially keen on Dot. She was a charmer. Everyone said so. I bet she could have even convinced them to lend her the accordion, if she had asked.

At first I thought I wouldn't tell Dot and Esther about the accordion. I think I might've said something about getting a piano over Christmas—like maybe for sure this was the year, and I didn't want to be reminded how wrong I was. But by Friday, when Dot rang our doorbell, I'd changed my mind. I felt entitled to a dose of pity.

On the way to school, while Sonia raced ahead of us, I told them about my grandfather's Camroni.

"You know what they say about accordions," Dot said. "If you go to heaven, God gives you a piano. If it's hell, then the devil's got an accordion waiting for you."

"Aw, *Daaawwwt!*" Esther practically bawled. "That's not even funny! 'Sides, what's so bad about the accordion? Once, my Papa found one thrown out with somebody's trash. We thought it was swell when he brought it home. He thought it looked awfully valuable, but when he opened it up, moths flew out of the bellows. I guess it's in our living room somewhere, but I wouldn't know where to start digging."

Dot sniffed. January made our noses run, but nobody wanted to stop in the cold to fish around for a handkerchief. "So what's he like?" asked Dot, sniffing and changing the subject.

"Who?"

"Your new teacher, silly. Gioseff DeMarco." She said his name in a grand sort of way and gave me a soft punch in the arm.

I shivered. Now I knew I should've kept my mouth closed. It was too cold to talk. I envied Esther's trousers, and wished Mamma would sew me a pair. But she never sewed boy's clothes. Not even for money. It was some private rule with her.

"Nice...I think." I hated to admit it, but it was true.

I told them about how he played "Ciribiribin" and made goofy, big-brotherish faces at Sonia and Emelina when my parents weren't looking. I told about the missing fingers, which Dot thought was very mysterious. And I told them my first lesson was tomorrow.

"Well, if you ask me, I think it's great!" said Dot brightly. "I'd love to have a boy coming round my house every Saturday morning."

"Gioseff's not a boy. If you like him so much, why don't you learn accordion!" I shot back.

I couldn't believe it. Well—and then I sort of could. Dot was a bit boy crazy. Every boy in our class, she thought, might be worthy of going around with one day. Except for Dennis Lister. She hated Dennis Lister. We all hated Dennis Lister. He was just this sinewy weasel of a kid— just a tight bundle of snotty, mean expressions, which streamed out of his mouth like a polluted river overflowing its banks. Dennis Lister was a kid most foul. He knew every racial slur for every kid at Strathcona School—*Jap*, *Chink*, *Kraut*, *Hunky*, *Wop*—and he used them all. I didn't know much about him, except that he was new to the neighborhood that year. When he wasn't in the chair facing the corner for saying something like "Miss Pringle has shingles" he sat right behind me in class. It was juss-a my kind-a luck to sit near him. He had holes in the soles of his shoes. Once, in the cloakroom, I saw him stuff cardboard in one shoe, to fill it in. He always stank because he never took a bath—or almost never. Sometimes it got so bad that Miss Pringle had to poke a finger in his back and march him downstairs to the basement, where there was a bathtub for the kids who never washed at home.

"Hah! No way!" barked Dot. "I'll take my chances on a piano at the Pearly Gates, thank you very much. Besides, all week long I'd have to practice, practice, practice, and then my parents would make me do stupid Christmas concerts in the living room for the rellies and then—wouldn't I just want to die? I mean, wouldn't you?" she asked us.

Esther said yes, she hadn't thought of that, but Dot had to be right. Playing "I Had a Little Dreidle" on the accordion for her grandparents at Hanukkah would surely be the end of her. She could imagine nothing more mortifying, besides maybe getting chased home from school by Dennis Lister wielding a handful of rocks and a slingshot.

So much for sympathy. I'd never even thought to dread accordion concerts in the living room. Now I had a whole new nightmare. Because just when you think things look bad enough, is right about the time they get worse. And isn't that the truth?

CHAPTER 6
How to Not Get Your Prayer Answered

"MARIANGELA?" whispered Sonia from her bed next to mine.

"Yes," I said, staring at the ceiling.

"You awake?"

"I think so."

"Good. I have a new prayer for you."

"What?"

"It goes like this:

"*Now I lay me down to sleep,*

"*I pray the Lord, my soul to keep,*

"*That I won't die before I wake,*

"*I pray the Lord my 'cordion to take.*

"What do you think?"

"Uh, huh. It's perfect. Thanks a lot," I said flatly.

"You're welcome. Anytime." She rolled over to face Emelina's side of the room, the direction she always slept in. And just like that, she fell asleep.

I listened to my sisters' breathing in the darkened bedroom. Emelina's breath came and went a little faster than Sonia's, but they fit together. Even though Emelina had only been moved from her crib in Mamma and Papa's room to her "big girl" bed in our room a few weeks earlier, I couldn't remember what it was like before, when I could only hear Sonia sleep. Emelina was a deep sleeper—so deep that she fell out of her bed a couple times a week. She'd wake us with a loud mew, like a cat that had hit the floor. And then, while Sonia and I bickered over whose turn it was to get up and tuck her back in, Emelina would curl up, there on the rug, and go back to sleep.

Everyone knows a prayer doesn't take unless you say it on chilled knees, at the foot of your bed, in the January cold of an unheated bedroom. God likes that kind of effort. But I guess by then I was resigned to the next day's lesson. I stayed in bed, hugging my hot water bottle to my chest, and recited the prayer that Sonia had composed for me.

I wasn't really surprised to see the accordion waiting at the foot of my bed when I woke up the next morning. God had not taken it in the night. It was still there, like Mamma's suitcase— packed and ready to go.

Gioseff rang our doorbell promptly at 10:30 on Saturday morning. I answered it while Mamma made a fuss of shooing Emelina and Sonia out of the living room. Papa stayed in the kitchen with his newspaper. Everyone pretended they weren't listening so hard that the house ached with the strain of their effort.

Gioseff wore his accordion over his shoulder, like a satchel. Papa had set up a little black music stand in the living room and brought the

Camroni downstairs. Gioseff swung his accordion off and set it on the carpet. It was as big as mine, with the same number of keys and buttons. And on the gleaming black grille was boldly proclaimed the name of its maker: Scandalli.

Gioseff pulled the footstool out for me to sit on and took the sofa for himself. Then he leaned forward, reached out, and took my right hand in his. "One, two, three, four, five," he said, counting down, beginning with the thumb as he folded my fingers into a fist.

"That's what you need to remember. Thumb is number one. Pinky is five.

"You ready now?"

I just sat there dumbly, which I knew from experience was the same to a teacher as "Yes." He slid into his accordion and motioned for me to do the same. At first I tried to lift it, but it was too heavy. I grunted and felt tears sting my eyes.

"No, no—like this." Gioseff picked up the accordion in one hand, set it on the sofa, and showed me how to slip into it. "Now, straighten up. If you stand like a chicken, your back will get tired fast."

I tried to tuck my behind in, but it was hard to stay balanced. Already my face was flushed and sweaty, and I hadn't even played a note.

"Standing makes playing easier. You can walk with it. Pace it out with your steps. Here, you sit for now, and I'll show you something."

He did. Something Spanish-sounding. I could almost see dancers in the room—swirling red and black peasant skirts, snapping their fans, clicking their heels—and Gioseff played as if he danced along with them.

I think he thought that would cheer me up, but I just felt more discouraged by his perform-ance. I could not understand how his left and right hand worked together, or how he could keep pumping the bellows in between. It was baffling.

"Listen, we start simple. You forget about the

left hand, just learn the right. Your thumb and middle C start here—one-two-three-four-five, cross over six-seven-eight." He demonstrated a scale and I tried to copy him; but I kept forgetting to push and pull the bellows. Without air, the accordion made no sound. Frustrated, I'd push a key again and again, as if it were broken, and then remember that I hadn't moved the bellows.

"Okay, forget the keys then," said Gioseff, with obvious patience. "We start by making it breathe."

"Slow open, slow close. Slow open, slow close," Gioseff repeated, over and over. On its own, I could do that—just make it breathe. I pushed and pulled maybe thirty times, and then he added the C key. He held his down with his thumb, I held mine, breathed in, then out, open, closed. Next D. Slow open, slow close—E...

By the end of the hour, I had a scale. I could get up to the top, and down again. Not smoothly, but in fits and starts, like the breathing. My accordion sounded asthmatic. My scale was not an elegant, rippling trill like Cousin Gigi played on the piano, but a stumbling ascent from C to C. To me, the difference between reaching the summit of the scale and falling off the mountain altogether seemed only a hair's breadth apart. My fingers stumbled a few steps up the keyboard and then tripped over themselves when I should've crossed over with my thumb. But each time I fell off the scale, Gioseff, the leader of the expedition, repeated gently, "Just keep going; don't fall off."

At the end of it, my face and hands were damp with sweat. Gioseff showed me how to slip off the accordion the way I'd put it on. When it came to taking it off, I was a quick learner.

"Mariangela, do you like the accordion?" he asked simply. "The sound, I mean."

I didn't dare answer it aloud. I could hear Papa rustling his paper in a very obvious just-pretend-I'm-not-here way. I just shook my head. I'm sure the look on my face said enough.

"Well, listen," said Gioseff, lowering his voice to a hush. "I can't make you like to play it; but I think, if you learn even a little, you will hear more in the music than you can today. There is something about the accordion. It needs air. It breathes just like you and I do. You learn to breathe with it, and how you feel when you play it expands like the bellows. You feel sad—it'll cry with you. You feel happy—it'll lead the dance. Tired? It lifts you up. You want to celebrate, clap your hands, give a present—the accordion can do all that for you. You only have to ask her right.

"That's what I'm here to teach you. How to ask her right."

He cleared his throat and called out, "I think that's enough for today."

My father was in the room as quick as the flick of a light switch. He held out an envelope to

Gioseff and then saw him to the door. They exchanged a few words while I tried to get the Camroni back in its box.

"Mariangela," called Gioseff, from the hallway, "You know where the best place for an accordion is?"

I didn't.

"Out of its case!" he said cheerfully. "See you next week!"

See you.

CHAPTER 7
English and Geography

IT WAS PAPA who drew the boundaries of English and Italian. It happened after I came home crying from my first day at kindergarten. I hadn't understood the teacher. I hadn't understood most of the other kids. Languages encircled me, like schools of fish, and English was the sea they all seemed to swim in. Except for me. I didn't know any English. Until then, we had only spoken Italian at home.

When Papa came home from work that night, he wanted to hear all about my first day. I told him I didn't understand the other kids, and worse, I didn't understand the teacher. I told him I was too afraid to ask to go to the bathroom, and I wet my pants on the way home. Papa was not one for decrees and orders. But from that day on, he insisted we speak English in the house.

For a while Mamma tried to keep up with the rest of us. She learned that "Good morning!" was what to say to Mrs. Pomeroy, who lived next door, when they were hanging out the first laundry of the day. And "Good evening!" was for when they met again in the late afternoon to draw in their lines.

By my fifth Christmas, I had a complete wardrobe of words, which brought me Dot and Esther. The three of us were consumed by the daily kindergarten ritual of show and tell. Dot brought in photographs of her relatives in England, ribbons, and a lock of pepper-and-salt fur from her dog, Smoky. Because her parents were always collecting, Esther had no shortage of things to choose from: pictures with broken frames, a sparkling paste diamond earring without a mate, a cracked teacup, a pocket-watch without hands...

Mostly, I brought in toys: a stuffed dog, a tiny doll as long as my baby finger, and a wooden hammer and peg set, made by Papa—first for me, but later used with much more relish by Sonia. Every time I wanted to bring something for show and tell, I had to ask Mamma first. She was very strict about me keeping my things nice.

"Mamma, can I take this to school?" I'd plead.

"*Perché?* (Why?)"

"Show'n tell!"

Mamma would always answer that it was fine, although she confused me a little because she always said something like, *Wasn't I a nice girl to always be thinking of show and tell?* But one time, I guess I'd asked too often, and she got frustrated.

"Who is this Showen Tell?" Mamma asked. "Doesn't she have her own toys? Can't Dot or Esther lend her something once in a while?"

And then I got it that Mamma hadn't

understood me for months. So I broke Papa's rule, which I followed even when he wasn't in earshot, and explained in Italian. It was silly; we should have laughed, but Mamma looked ashamed. After that I didn't check with her about show and tell anymore. Papa and I, and even Sonia, were swimming fast in the English current; Mamma was still back on the Italian shore. I didn't like leaving her behind, and I didn't want to remind her of how far out I'd managed to swim without her.

As the winter settled upon my kindergarten year, Mamma stayed mostly indoors. Our laundry dried on a clothes rack in the kitchen, (no more daily trials to talk to the neighbors putting out the wash), and she withdrew to her sewing and the company of her own familiar words. She sewed in Italian. I know, because that is what she spoke to the pieces of cloth as she cut and pinned and stitched.

My father did his swearing in our cowshed.

There were no cows there to hear him—nobody on our block had cows anymore, although there were a few here and there in the neighborhood. I liked cows. We had kindred eyes.

In our house, there were strict rules about who could say what where. The borders around cursing territory were very narrow. Mamma permitted Papa's gutter talk only in the cowshed. That was where he seemed to need it most anyway, as it was his place for hammering things out.

Papa's first loyalty to Italian swearing never wavered. Whether it was because he respected Mamma's rule, or his own, the cowshed was foul language *centrale* (central). Still, sound traveled. We could hear him if we opened our bedroom back window. Sonia and Emelina especially loved the sound of words doubly forbidden, and would silently mouth them to each other: *Managgia! Merdoso! Porca miseria! Porco cane!*

To hear Papa in the cowshed, you would think his carpentry projects—mostly tables, stools, and cupboards that he made for extra money—were one torturous disaster after another. In fact, though, my father was known not for his cowshed mouth but for the simple, smooth furniture he built, one cuss word at a time.

The day after my first accordion lesson, words came from the cowshed: Papa had a new project. He worked quickly all that Sunday afternoon and, just before dinner, called up to my bedroom window for me to come down and see what he had made.

It was a wagon. Black wheels with round, white hubcaps and plain wood fencing. He'd made Sonia a much smaller one, as a birthday present, a few years before. She used it to bring milk back from the store for Mamma. Had Papa forgotten I was eleven? Too old to pull dolls in a wagon, outgrown the milk chore.

"You can take your accordion to Gioseff's," Papa explained. "He's gonna teach you at his house from now on. Tuesdays. After school."

I felt the shame, of things to come, rush up and make my face burn red. Now the whole neighborhood would see me dragging my accordion up the street. Mothers pushing baby prams would give me sympathetic looks. Fathers shoveling coal into wheelbarrows at the curbside would say to their sons, "Look at that poor Benetti kid; her parents are makin' her learn accordion." Little kids would point and pick their noses. I would be a new spectacle on Union Street—something to laugh over at the dinner table.

What did Papa expect me to say? *Thank you*? Well, then he expected too much. Instead, like lightning out of a bottle, I heard my voice cuss a blue streak of Italian that cut the sawdust-air in the dappled light of the cowshed and shocked both of us.

"*Odio questa maledetta fisarmonica!*"

Too far. I'd gone too far.

Papa's face flinched, then froze stone cold. I was lucky he wasn't a smacker. My parents never hit any of us. When they got mad, they got quiet and pretended we weren't there. It was awful. Dot had gotten the wooden spoon a couple of times from her mother. She said it stung, but in her house that was it: no confession to wait for, no silent meals. It was over and done with. The silent treatment was scarier; you never quite knew when it would end.

Papa's eyes flashed angrily at first, but then I thought I saw a spark of something else, like he was holding down a smile. "I'll paint it up nice. What color would you like? Green? Blue? Yellow?"

The cowshed had no heat, and suddenly I became aware of how cold it was. I just wanted to get back inside. I pulled my cardigan tight around me and stuck my hands in my armpits. When I breathed out, a faint cloud formed in front of my face. I scanned the shelf above Papa's head, where the paint cans were stored. My eyes followed a shaft of light that came through the shed's only window to land, like a spotlight, on a can of bright red paint. The opposite of camouflage is red. The color of swearing is red. When you are right up against it, the only color is red. I pointed to the can with the streaks of carmine that had drip-dried down its sides.

"Red's good," I said, numbed out by my swearing fit, and still wary that Papa might have a delayed reaction.

Papa reached for the tin. "Better go help your mother with dinner," he said, poking around for a clean paintbrush.

"And, Mariangela?"

I turned back.

"Don't ever let your mother hear you use words like that."

CHAPTER 8

Good for the Luck

IT RAINED ON TUESDAY AFTERNOON, beginning just as school let out and pouring by the time I got home. Dot and Esther wanted to hang around and walk with me to my lesson. Dot was keen to have a good, close-up look at Gioseff, but the cold rain put off dawdling for another day. They abandoned me at the door just as Mamma came outside, lugging the accordion case.

The wagon was at the bottom of the steps. She lifted the accordion onto the wagon, quickly gave me the dollar for Gioseff, and hurried back inside.

It was only three blocks, two up, one across, to Mrs. Secco's boarding house, where Gioseff had a room. I was glad of the rain. Everyone was indoors, busy and warm, as I trudged up the street. The curbs were hard and slowed me down; I had to stop, lower the front of the wagon onto the road, holding the accordion for balance, and ease the back wheels down. Then it was the same again on the other side. I looked in the front windows of houses I passed—Mamma always told me that it was rude, but I couldn't help myself. I wanted to see who had a radio. Radios were a real luxury in our neighborhood. The only people I knew with radios were Uncle Tony and Esther. But Esther's didn't really count because her father had scavenged it broken, and hadn't ever gotten around to getting it fixed.

A couple of bored little kids pressed wet noses against windows and watched me go by. I turned the corner and felt the accordion case tip a little behind me. When I turned back to steady it, I glanced up at another window. The face staring back gave me a chill: it was Dennis Lister. He was glaring down from the top floor of Mrs. Porchenski's boarding house. I knew he lived with his father around here somewhere. No one knew where his mother was, or had ever met her. Some kids said she was a ghost, haunting the Mountain View cemetery; others had heard she was wooed away to San Francisco by a sailor. Either way, we were sure she was gone for good. We figured that Dennis wasn't the kind of kid you came back for.

As I passed Mrs. Porchenski's, Dennis swung the window open and yelled out, "Hey, Waaaawwwp! Hey, you Daaaayyygo!" The words he relished saying were beaten down by the rain, but I knew what he said, since he'd called me this often enough in the cloakroom at school.

"Hey, you greasy Gypsy! You runnin' away to join the circus? Gonna tell fortunes?"

My hand pulling the wagon had gone numb. The freezing rain sopped through my mitten. I stopped just long enough to switch the wagon handle with my other hand.

I hadn't understood why Dennis liked calling me a Gypsy, until Esther told me it was because of my earrings. I was the only girl in our class who had earrings—tiny golden teardrops with flower engravings. My ears had been pierced back before my remembering began, because, according to Nonna, a girl should start life with a little gold in each ear. "Good fo' da luck!" she said, when it came time to do Emelina's. That, I remember.

Nonna was so quick with the needle that Emelina didn't start shrieking and crying until she'd done her second ear. Mamma held Emelina on her lap and smoothed the betrayed expression from her face. Sonia and I watched the whole thing with horrified fascination.

I secretly liked my earrings. They were my own precious treasure at a time when nobody had much of anything. But Nonna was wrong, I thought, as I pulled the wagon to a stop in front of Mrs. Secco's. What had they brought me so far? Luck hadn't singled me out for any special goodness. My earrings caught only the sneers of Dennis Lister. My gold could only have come from cursed ground.

CHAPTER 9

If You Have no Shoes to Eat, There Are Always Cookies

THAT NIGHT AT THE DINNER TABLE, Papa asked me how the lesson went. I had already shown Sonia the beginner's sheet music Gioseff had given me, with the publisher's bold promise: *Learn the accordion for fun and profit! A lifetime of pleasure and a profitable career await the trained musician! Parents, give your family the gift of music—the melodious tones of an accordion—a complete orchestra in a box!*

I handed the music to Papa and showed him the scales inside.

"More scales?" he asked. "No song yet?" When I said, no, just exercises, he pretended to be mildly disappointed.

"Well, never mind. It's only your second

week. Practice in the living room after dinner. We want to hear what you've learned."

I had just finished telling them about Mrs. Secco's parlor, where we had the lesson—how the walls were wallpapered with yellow flowers, how the rug and all the parlor furniture were yellow, too—when Sonia pulled a note out of her pocket and handed it to Mamma. Even though Mamma couldn't read, it was the ritual in our family that all notes from school went to her first. She opened it and studied the page for a moment before handing it to me with a sigh.

I recognized the small, tight handwriting of Sonia's teacher, Miss Snively. Sonia was unconcerned, and in her usual way calmly ate her ravioli and green beans while she waited for me to begin. Since September, we'd had other notes from Miss Snively:

Sonia is a distraction to the other children.

Sonia is a chatterbox who cannot seem to control her giggling.

Sonia has been passing notes again.

Sonia has been speaking Italian in class.

"Use your fork," said Mamma to Emelina, who was poking green beans into her mouth with her fingers. *"E allora, Mariangela,"* she said, turning to me, *"cosa dice questa volta* (So, what does it say this time)?"

It seemed Miss Snively had a problem with breakfast—at least, she did with Sonia's.

I did my best to assume Miss Snively's snippy voice:

Dear Mrs. Benetti,

During our lesson this morning on human nutrition, it came to my notice that Sonia's diet is <u>remarkably</u> unsuitable for a growing child. I am particularly concerned by Sonia's claim of <u>eating cookies</u> and <u>drinking coffee</u> at breakfast. While given her frequent inclinations toward exaggeration there is, of course, a possibility that I should doubt her testimony, I feel it is my duty to draw the issue to your attention.

Coffee and *cookies* are simply not a whole-some breakfast for a growing child. They are lacking in substance and the general nutrients necessary to a healthy disposition. Nor does this set a good example for Sonia's classmates (over whom she seems to have some influence). I would be happy to lend you several instructional textbooks on this subject; you have only to ask and I shall send them home with Sonia.

In the meantime, may I respectfully suggest porridge, toast, and orange juice for Sonia as a better morning meal?

Yours truly,

Miss Lydia Snively

At first I thought my mother didn't understand the letter. Miss Snively liked big, superior words. I looked at Papa.

"Mamma, do you want me to translate it?"

Mamma shook her head. She understood enough to look wounded.

"Sonia, what's this all about?" Papa asked.

Sonia put her fork down and finished chewing.

"Miss Snively asked us to draw pictures of everything we ate yesterday. Every meal. Bobby Horwood, next to me, didn't draw breakfast or lunch. All he had was soup and bread for dinner. Miss Snively tapped her pointer finger on his picture for a long time and didn't say anything. Fumiko Yamaguchi drew soup for her breakfast, but it was weird looking; it had little white cubes floating into it. That made Miss Snively kind of annoyed. Then, with me, she tapped her finger on the *caffé latte* and biscotti I'd drawn for breakfast. She asked me, 'Is that coffee? Does your mother give you cookies for breakfast?' I told her, 'Yes, but only on Saturdays.' Her face pinched down really tight, and she marched to her desk and wrote the note out.

"She came back with the note and told me, 'Cookies are a bad breakfast, Sonia. No wonder you're getting fat. You take this home to your mother.' And she slapped the note down on my picture."

In a mean way, Miss Snively was a little bit right. Sonia was softer and rounder than the rest of us. Every time she visited, Nonna reassured herself that Sonia "still got her baby fat." Uncle Tony called her "the wrestler." But in our house, all this was praise. Nobody ever bothered Sonia with "You so skinny! Why you no eat?"

Mamma looked dejected. We sat there for a moment and then, from Papa, came a soft "Heh, heh, heh, heh—" that grew until he had to push his chair back from the table, he was laughing so hard.

"Miss Snively, she probably thinks a good breakfast is sucking on a lemon every morning," said Papa, making a sour face. "This note? I'll show you where it goes—"

We all watched as he leaned over, lifted the note from my fingers, crumpled it up, opened the oven door, and tossed it in. Then he came back to the table and kissed Mamma on the cheek.

"Girls, you're so lucky to have such a cook in your mother! And so much food in one house. Enough for my whole village in Italy!" he boasted. "When I was a boy, we were so poor and so hungry all the time that one day, I ate my shoes!"

We all started laughing, Emelina squirming in her seat with happiness at one of Papa's favorite jokes. Even Mamma smiled. We knew it so well that we added the next part for him:

"But Papa, you didn't have shoes!" we cried, and, without missing a beat, Papa chimed in, "Not after I ate them!"

In that moment, Miss Snively's dark spell over Mamma was broken. We laughed as if we all shared the secret of the universe. And it was very good.

CHAPTER 10
Flavia's Invitation

I PRACTICED IN THE LIVING ROOM for a week, thunking up and down scales with my right hand, missing notes altogether when I forgot to press the bellows. After the week was out, Papa said maybe it was okay if I practiced upstairs instead. He made me a wooden stool to sit on. After dinner I'd head for the staircase, and Mamma would call after me, "Mariangela, make sure the window's closed, okay?"

A few times, Emelina came in and tried to press the keys while I played, but usually she grabbed her baby blanket from her bed and stomped out with a crabby "I'm going to the bathroom to take a nap!"

With my right hand, the scales were beginning to take hold. Gioseff said that my hands had memory; so did my arms, my legs. It wasn't just the head that remembered—the body kept memories, too. Practice was about training my fingers to remember how to move to make music. It seemed after a few weeks that it might be true about my right hand, but my left was definitely a goofball. I could find the grooved C-note button, but I couldn't remember to play it in quarter notes as I moved up the scale. At home, I let the left lag, and just worked on going up and down with my right. It was better than getting nowhere using both hands together.

Finally, after four Tuesday lessons, Gioseff decided that I was ready to learn a song. He played "On Top of Old Smoky" from my music book, but he couldn't resist some flourishes to dress it up. He made it sound like a show tune, not the song we learned in kindergarten. I tried to pick out the melody with my right hand, while Gioseff made the quarter notes and chords for me. For a brief second, I thought I recognized the melody.

Sometimes I could get all the way home from Gioseff's without Dennis screeching at me from his window.

"Hey, you gar*lick*-eater! Hey, Olive Oyl! Hey, polenta girl! Hey, Waaaaaaaaaaaaaaawwp! You gonna play me a tune? Or just run away to the circus?"

Once, I heard a sharp, snapping sound hailing against my case, just as I was passing Mrs. Porchenski's. I looked up and saw Dennis, in his lookout, loading a slingshot with pebbles. He dropped down like an enemy soldier with his cover blown, and I made it past without him taking another shot.

I never told anyone about Dennis. I didn't even spill the beans to Sonia, in case it got back to Mamma. Besides, what could my mother do? She couldn't even scare him in a language he'd understand. Besides, I didn't want him laughing in anyone else's face. All Mamma knew was that I didn't like Dennis Lister from up the street. I figured the less she knew, the safer she was. He was a kid who could fling the crap far.

The day after the "Old Smoky" lesson, I came home to find Mamma with Signora Antonelli and her daughter, Flavia, in the living room. Flavia was getting fitted for her wedding dress. Flavia had large eyes and thick, curling eyelashes that gave her a sweet baby-doll face. She had long, wavy black hair that she wore off her face. Too bad for her, she also had a double chin. Flavia rounded out where other women curved in. I thought she looked like a doll that had been made out of gnocchi. She was nice, and she always brought us a box of cream-filled cannoli from her father's bakery when she came for a fitting.

Flavia teetered on a tiny footstool in the middle of the living room. She looked a little sweaty from the strain of keeping her balance.

"Hi, Mariangela!" said Flavia, trying to hold her stomach in. "Your Mamma says you're learning the accordion?"

Flavia's dress was almost finished. Mamma had done such a nice job you could barely see where her stomach poked out. Flavia looked pleased, but Mamma was frowning over the waist-line—she thought it looked too tight. Letting it out would be a problem—even I knew that. The old stitchmarks would show in the satin. Mamma tried to explain this to Flavia and Mrs. Antonelli, but I don't think Flavia was listening.

"You think maybe you could play something at my wedding?" Flavia asked me.

I was shocked. Mamma obviously had not told her that all I could play were scales.

"I can't play any songs yet. Only scales."

"Well, there's still a month to go! You could learn something by then. Sure you can!" Flavia seemed very excited by the idea. "It'll be fun, everybody will love it. Maybe your mother can make you a new dress!"

I thought Flavia had to be crazy. For sure she was going to be sorry. Even if I did learn a song, who would want "On Top of Old Smoky" at their wedding? My mother tugged at the waistline again and said something I could barely hear, about how another month and she'd have to make a whole new dress. Mrs. Antonelli winced, like Mamma had just stuck a pin in her cheek, and Flavia blushed like she'd been dipped in red wine. Mamma glanced up to see them exchange startled silent looks. She patted her blonde coronet, something she did when she was thinking, and then, as deftly as the needle she slipped through satin, she turned the attention onto me.

"I think it's a good idea, Mariangela. Gioseff can teach you something. You let him know you need a song for a wedding. He'll know what it should be."

The Antonelli ladies relaxed and the color faded from Flavia's face.

"It'll be fun!" Flavia called cheerfully, as I excused myself. "You'll see. You'll get all dressed up and be so cute. It'll be swell!"

Careful what you wish for—that was Dot's saying. She got it from her mother, who used it all the time. Too bad for Flavia; somebody should have taught her to be careful about her wishes.

Later that night, I found Mamma in the sewing room, adding panels into the sides of Flavia's wedding dress. "Too much *gelato*, that one," she said, with a don't-even-so-much-as-ask-me look on her face, as she ripped open the seams.

CHAPTER 11

Santa Maria Accordiana

AT MY NEXT CONFESSION, Father Paul gave me three Hail Marys for swearing in the cowshed. He explained that it wasn't so much the words I used as raising my voice in anger at my father—*that* was a couple of sins combined.

"Examine your conscience carefully," Father Paul prompted every week through the screened partition. Usually I didn't come up with much— maybe a fight with Sonia over cutting up the paper before she had a chance to see it. So it was almost a relief to have something this time.

I told Father Paul about the accordion, about Gioseff, about envying Cousin Gigi her piano… I'm not sure he was really listening. I think he was concentrating more on adding up the right price tag for the swearing.

"Mariangela, you must look into your heart. Genuine contrition is the path to atonement," said Father Paul when I had finished. "Is it your true will not to make this sin again?"

"Yes, Father Paul."

Then, he told me that I must be a good and obedient daughter. If my parents wanted me to learn music, if they wanted me to practice, then that was my duty to them and to God. God, it seemed, was clearly on the side of the accordion.

"God loves you for your sincere apology," said Father Paul as I got up and pushed the curtain aside. As I stepped out into the aisle, so did Father Paul. He was very tall, with gray hair and glasses. Older than Papa. It was hard to face him, straight on, after confessing. I looked down at the carpet and shifted on my feet.

"Just a moment, Mariangela," Father Paul went up to the organ and opened the bench. He took out a hymnbook and flipped through the pages until he found what he was looking for.

"No Hail Marys after all. Learn this on the accordion instead." He pointed to the song in the book: "Alleluia."

"God would be pleased; you can play it for the congregation at Easter," said Father Paul, closing the book and handing it to me. Then he walked back to the confessional and disappeared behind the curtain.

On the way home, Sonia walked with me, while Mamma and Papa were ahead, swinging Emelina between them.

"I think I need a saint," I said to Sonia glumly.

"Wha' fo'?" said Sonia, having fun with the way Nonna would say it, without the *r*.

"For this accordion thing. People want me to play stuff. Flavia wants me to play at her wedding, Father Paul wants me to play at Mass."

"Really?" said Sonia. She sounded a bit impressed. "What does he want you to play?"

"'Alleluia.'"

"Yup, you're in trouble," said Sonia earnestly.

"The thing is, I don't think there are any saints of accordions."

Sonia knew her saints. It was her favorite part of catechism class. She cataloged them in her mind, by name and patronage. Some of her first scrapbooks were made up mostly of prayer cards of saints. She had cards of the patron saints for bakers, candle makers, pawnbrokers, difficult children, crippled people, maids, poets, and singers. It seemed near everyone had a patron saint. There were saints for places, saints to keep you safe, saints if you were in jail, and saints to keep you out of it. Mamma kept a small color picture of Saint Cabrini, patron saint of immigrants, on top of her dresser. Even Canada had Saint Anne—we learned about her in history; she was patron saint of the voyageurs. There were countless conditions to have, or avoid; and there was a saint for every day and everyone— except for the accordion.

"Are you sure?" I asked, but I knew she was

right. I'd gone through my *Lives of the Saints* book, and nowhere did the accordion show up. But Sonia was the expert in our family. When she was six, she insisted the new baby be called Emelina, after the Blessed Emilina—a nun with a gift for prophecy. Sonia thought this gift might be good to have in a little sister; but so far, our Emelina lived strictly in the moment. As we walked home, I watched her swinging between Mamma and Papa, counting, "One, two, three-eeeeeee," before they lifted her up and swung her forward, shrieking with delight, like the baby monkey she often pretended to be.

"Positive. Definitely there's no Santa Maria Accordiana. But let's see...how about Saint Cecilia? She's for musicians, especially church music. Or Gregory the Great? Musicians and schoolchildren pray to him. Or maybe Seraphina?"

"Who does she protect?"

"She was the beautiful hermit who lived her life in constant pain. She sewed and prayed a lot and gave to the poor, even though she was poor herself. There was always someone worse off than her, and she found a way to help them. Crippled people pray to her."

"So, she was poor and she hurt all the time?"

"Yeah, but at least her dad didn't make her play an accordion. It's kinda like you're one of those people she helped—one who had it worse than she did."

"Thanks a lot."

"You're welcome," said Sonia nonchalantly. That was one of my favorite words for Sonia— *nonchalant.* I found it in the newspaper once, then I cut it out and pasted it into one of her scrapbooks.

Just before bed that night, I settled on Saint Cecilia. I didn't want to think that I was even worse off than Saint Seraphina—the martyr who died a glorious death. That made me shudder, but so many of them ended up like that. I began the prayer in my book "Lord, hear my request. Through the intercession of Cecilia, please grant what I ask..."

...before I realized that I had forgotten what I was asking for.

CHAPTER 12

Who Is Dorothy Dix?

THE NEXT MORNING AT SCHOOL, Dot decided it wasn't a saint I needed. She sent me a note in the middle of spelling. It was folded up as small as my pinkie nail:

Mariangela, I have an IDEA!!! Why don't you write to DOROTHY DIX about your accordion?!!??!! Maybe SHE could give you some advice on how to GET OUT of it?!!??!!

Dorothy Dix was the answer lady in the newspaper. People wrote to her with their questions. Mostly it was housewives who had fallen in love with their sisters' husbands, or husbands who didn't want to talk business with their wives, or parents who had pesky grown-up kids who only came home for money.

Dot didn't read the rest of the paper, but she

read Dorothy Dix every day. I didn't. She was too boring. Sonia thought that Dorothy Dix was snippety Miss Snively's secret identity. Mamma just didn't read at all. But one day before Christmas, Aunt Letizia confessed that she wrote to Dorothy Dix about how to get cousin Giulietta to stop running around in the nude. Giulietta lived to strip and to streak past Gigi at the piano, through Zia Letizia's kitchen, and out onto the porch. Everyone knew she was trying to make it to the street; but the stairs slowed her down just enough, and she always got caught. Even in the middle of February, Giulietta would squirm around in her dress, itching for the satisfaction of a good fast streak.

Giulietta was three, like Emelina, so it wasn't too shocking really. But I think the nude thing must have stumped Dorothy Dix, because Aunt Letizia never got her free advice. Instead, Uncle Tony added special locks to the front and back doors of their house, to make it harder for Giulietta to get outside.

So I didn't have a lot of faith in getting a reply. But still, Dot's idea rang in my head all morning. All I could think about in school was what I'd say in the letter. At lunchtime, I went home and wrote it out while a bowl of vegetable soup cooled in front of me. Only Sonia ate. Emelina was too busy running back and forth from the kitchen to the living room in only her undershirt. Lately she'd been trying to keep out of clothes, something Mamma was sure she'd picked up from Cousin Giulietta.

Dear Dorothy Dix,

I wanted a piano for Christmas, but I didn't get it. Instead, my grandmother gave me my grandfather's clunky old accordion, and now my parents have signed me up for lessons. I think this is really unfair. And it's heavy too! It's got to weigh the same as my little sister, Emelina, who is three, at least when she has no clothes on, which is a lot of the time these days since my Aunt Letizia wrote to you

before Christmas about how our cousin
Giulietta always runs around nude and
shocks the neighbors but you never wrote back
and so now Emelina has started it too and my
mother chases her around saying,
"O SIGNORE… VESTITI!" which basically
means God help me, put some clothes on! in
case you don't speak Italian, which I do,
except not at home because my father is pretty
strict about speaking good English or he says
we'll bring shame to the family and never get
anywhere in this country.

Anyway, I want to quit the accordion, but
I know my parents won't let me. No way! Do
you have any advice? Please answer my question and I will read you every day, I promise.

Yours very truly,

Mariangela Benetti

P.S. My best friend Dot is your biggest fan.
She doesn't have a boyfriend but she reads
your column every day so that she'll be ready.

*She really liked how you said boys should
treat girls nicely and not act like they're God's
gift and not be sloppy or paw them and only
talk about themselves all the time or be bossy
or tell a girl how much lipstick she* ~~can~~ *may
use. But she thinks you were wrong about
how they shouldn't buy girls presents all the
time, she's not sure that's so bad of a thing.
Anyway, she says you're right on the money
about how if a boy looks like something the
cat brought in a girl won't step out with it.
Dot has her standards very clear in her head,
and they sound a lot like yours.*

I thought it was a pretty good letter, but it
took me almost the whole hour to write it. There
was no time to find an envelope, and I'd have to
ask Dot to lend me a penny for a stamp because
I couldn't ask Mamma, or I'd have to explain. So
I stuck it in my schoolbag, for later, and hurried
back.

After dinner that night, Sonia sat on the floor pasting an article into her scrapbook. It was about how Vancouver was going to have fourteen different committees to plan for the king and queen's visit. When she was done with the front page, she handed it up to Papa. He quietly studied the picture on the front page.

"Mariangela, come look at this," said Papa softly, pointing to the picture. "This little girl, she looks just like you."

The photograph was of a long, crowded line of children, wrapped in blankets and waiting in the cold, somewhere in the south of France. They were refugees of the Spanish Civil War, and they all looked sad and hungry.

"Look," said Papa, pointing to one girl with round cheeks and dark eyes, who stared straight at the camera. "Doesn't she look just like you? Carmella, look at this girl, doesn't she look just like our Mariangela?"

Mamma came and peered over Papa's shoulder. He explained that the children were fleeing France and Mamma looked sad. Day after day, we'd read in the paper that Spanish refugees were dying in air raids, as Generalissimo Franco's planes dropped bombs on the cities they'd fled to for safety.

"Dio, aiutali (God help them)," sighed Mamma, and she gave me a hug around the shoulders. Suddenly I felt guilty. The papers were full of news about how Jews were fleeing from Germany, and how signs on many German shops and hotels now read: Jews Forbidden. In Rome, the Pope was very sick and was expected to die any day. In Britain, people were taking air raid precautions, in case they came under attack.

My letter to Dorothy Dix was still in my schoolbag. I had the envelope I needed. And Esther had given me one of the uncanceled stamps that her mother saved from envelopes she sometimes found in the trash. But complaining about accordion lessons seemed silly then, with all that was going on in the world.

Papa was still looking at the picture.

"Maybe she does look like me," I said to Papa. I wasn't so sure, but I hoped he might smile if I agreed. "She's just missing her accordion."

And then I did a weird thing. I got up straightaway from the table, went upstairs, and took the letter out of my schoolbag. I tore out the stamp for saving and ripped the rest of the letter into little pieces. It could go in the oven, just like one of Miss Snively's notes. Then I heaved up the accordion, and clunked out "On Top of Old Smoky" until my fingers ached.

CHAPTER 13

The Truth According to Dennis Lister

"Hey, frog eyes!"

I kept going, staring at the pavement, as if only it could speak to me. Dennis still made me cringe inside, but I'd learned how to keep my spine straight.

"Frog Eye-talian!"

The slur seemed to fill the whole block. I tugged the wagon handle and started to hurry.

"You wanna know how come your teacher lost his fingers?"

I slowed down, only a little, not enough that I thought he'd notice. I hated to admit it, but I was curious.

"The Mafia! The MAFIA cut 'em off! That's

why he lives here now—he's hidin' out! But they're gonna find him; and when they do, they're gonna chop off the other ones, too!"

Dennis started to hoot. He sounded like a prisoner gone crazy.

I stopped and looked up at his window, from where he pelted rocks and words. God was supposed to send each of us a guardian angel, a good angel, to watch over us. But I felt like there'd been a mix-up in my case: I got a devil's imp—and his name was Dennis Lister. "Sticks and Stones" was such a lie. Bully words hurt the same as sticks and stones, just in different places.

The Mafia cut his fingers off? Gioseff's fingers—that had to be just boy gangster talk. It just had to! I wanted my mouth to fling something smart-ass, snappy, right back at Dennis. It would be a sin, but that wasn't what stopped me. The right words just came too slowly. My brain worked like a streetcar that never ran on time. It would catch up eventually, like just before I fell asleep on Sunday night. Then I'd know what I should've said days before.

I stood there, staring at Dennis, as he spat out the window into Mrs. Porchenski's flowerbed.

"So go chew on that with yer spaghetti dinner! Hah!" he blasted, and spat one more time. It was like his mouth was a BB gun and I was the gopher, right in his range. Mission accomplished, he slammed down the window.

The rest of the way home, I felt a little lump of uncertainty begin to grow inside me. Could it be true? Was Gioseff a criminal, mixed up with gangsters? Was he in danger? What if they came for him right in the middle of a lesson? Maybe I could chuck my accordion at them and knock them down the stairs. The accordion would land on top of the pile of them and crush them. Then it would be good for something.

After dinner that night, I sat in the kitchen and watched Mamma iron underwear. I liked watching the tidy piles grow, all our different sizes together—Emelina's doll-sized floral prints, my father's white undershirts and boxer shorts, Mamma's, Sonia's, mine. I liked that each little tower of underwear stood for one of us. And, if you tried to balance them too far apart, they fell over. But if one pile stood touching the next, they all stayed straight. Sometimes Mamma even ironed Emelina's doll clothes for Betsy Ann and Baby Bubbles: little organdy dresses and bonnets, bloomers and petticoats, even white silk ankle socks small enough to fit on your thumb.

"Mamma…"

"Mmmhmm?"

Should I tell her? For a half-second, I felt sorry for Dennis Lister, who had no mother to iron his underwear. Who had to take a bath at school, and never brought any lunch. Who had no accordion to pulverize his enemies with. No wonder he slung words. *Pulverize*. That was a great word. *Pulverize* was a comic-book-super-hero-strong word, like *smite* and *smote* and *smithereens*—I *smote* mine enemies with my trusty accordion.

Well, it was too late now; I had a word out and a toe in. Typically, I couldn't think of anything else to say fast enough for a cover. *Mafia* left a fearful, sour taste in my mouth. The word seemed almost unutterable. It felt like I was about to curse, right in front of my mother. I never told her about *Wop* or *Dago* or anything else Dennis Lister called me. First of all, I'd have to explain those words to her, and I didn't even know where they came from. And if Dennis said that's what I was, then she was, too. So it would be like spreading the meanness further.

If I didn't tell her, then she was protected. Wasn't that why she didn't learn English? To stay safe? Papa would know, and that made us allies. If those words got no farther than the sidewalk, if we didn't let them in the front door, then they weren't really about us. We could always hope they would be forgotten by morning, and never happen again.

Words out, toe in. Finish what you started, Mariangela.

"Mamma, Gioseff's fingers…you know, the missing ones?"

"Yes…," said Mamma slowly. She set her iron down.

"Were…were they were cut off by…the Mafia?"

My mother looked startled.

"Who told you that?"

"Dennis. Dennis Lister, from up the street…he…he said…he said that Gioseff's hiding out here, and when the Mafia find him, they'll cut the rest off!"

Mamma picked up the little stacks of underwear and handed them to me to take upstairs. Her full lips were pursed in a thin seam.

"What do you think, Mamma?"

She drew her brows together and looked me straight in the eyes.

"I don't know, Mariangela. Maybe he had an

accident. Maybe he had some trouble. Maybe he was born that way. But this one thing I know: it is better to ask the truth of someone, than to go around thinking lies."

Mamma turned back to the iron. For the moment, there was nothing more to say.

After that, I counted the days to my next lesson. I practiced left hand, right hand, and stomped around my room to mark the rhythm of pull and squeeze. The right-hand melody was getting easier. Sometimes I thought I recognized scraps of the tune Gioseff had played. But I couldn't get through the piece once, straight though, without some mistake that had me fall right out of the song.

I made up my mind right then, that night, in the kitchen with Mamma. I would ask Gioseff about his fingers. And when Tuesday came around, and he'd carried my case into Mrs. Porchenski's upstairs sitting room, I was ready. I'd say it fast and straight-out, Sonia-style. I wouldn't say it was none of my business; wouldn't squirm around like it was a big deal or I was scared, or I believed it or anything. I'd bunch the whole question up so dense that it would block the door and window, and he'd just *have* to tell me the truth.

Before he could open my case, it was out of me.

"Gioseff, Dennis Lister down the street, he said that the Mafia cut your fingers off. He said you were hiding out. And that when they found you, they'd come for the rest."

Gioseff looked dumbfounded.

My chest went tight. I was no Sonia, the breezy inquisitor. My question had been clumsy. Immediately I was awash in guilt.

"Whoa," he said under his breath. Leaving my accordion in its case, he sat down on the sofa. His face paled and he took a deep breath. His face wore a puzzled expression for another moment, and then he started to laugh—a low chuckle that lifted the corners of his mouth and lit up his eyes. He shook his head in disbelief.

"Mafia? Who knows Mafia? That's crazy. No, Mariangela, it wasn't anything like that at all." He paused.

"Do you want to know what happened?"

I nodded.

"You sure? The whole thing?"

I sat down on the worn needlepoint footstool, wrapped my arms around my knees and nodded again. Already I was fascinated; if not the Mafia, then what?

CHAPTER 14

What For a Pig

GIOSEFF SAID THAT IN A WAY, it all started with a pig. The pig his father raised when he was a boy. It was *his* pig. He fed it, and it grew fat and healthy. Gioseff's father thought that one day *his* father would butcher it for the family. There would be roasts, pancetta, chops, homemade sausages. But he never did. Instead, one summer, Gioseff's grandfather said, "Take this pig to the market, and see what you can get for it."

So Gioseff's father took the pig away. And he came back home with an accordion. A little squeeze box concertina that you held between your hands. He wore it home, slung over his shoulder on a leather strap.

Sure it was crazy, said Gioseff—especially then. If you had a pig, you ate it. Of course, they had other animals. The house where they lived was two stories. The ground was like a barn: sheep, goats, and chickens milled around over the dirt floor. In the winter this was good; the house was always warm because of the sheep. Their heat rose up through the floorboards. But there were mice there, too. You had to be careful not to get bit. The bite of a mouse could kill a man. *Veleno* (poison).

They always had food; they were better off than most. But they never had any *lire*. Gioseff's grandfather wasn't angry about the accordion. All he said was, "Fine. You learn to play it, then, or I trade it into a pig again."

So Gioseff's father learned. He learned by listening to the men in the village, who played at dances and weddings, in the market on Saturdays, or for their families at the end of the day. He watched their fingers and how their bodies moved. He copied the tunes into his mind and then figured them out, bit by bit, by himself.

As he got older, he started to get piecework from the accordion factory in the next town. He was mostly a reed maker, because those he could do at home. By the time his parents were married, Gioseff's father still worked on his grandfather's farm, but he had built a little house and his own workshop nearby. Just one floor, no sheep. So too bad for the DeMarcos; every winter they were very cold.

When Gioseff was about three, his father started to teach him the accordion. Not from music on paper—he couldn't even read Italian. He didn't even know that music could be written down. He learned what he listened to: little songs of the village, songs from the marketplace, from the traveling circus, from the man who made music for the dancing bear. Nothing with a name. Just "Mother's Song," or "Farewell Song," or "Song for Springtime," or "Village Dance." That sort of thing.

Gioseff's father died when he was forty. Gioseff was twelve; his brother Guillermo was almost sixteen. It was just a slip of his knife that started it. The boys never saw the accident; they were both at school. He was cutting a reed, and the knife went on from the stroke, followed through deep into his hand—a gashing cut. Little cuts, knife scratches, happened to him all the time. He almost never noticed them until *cena* (supper time). But this was no small nick. He came out of the workshop bleeding and calling for help. Gioseff's mother cleaned and bandaged his hand, but the bandage quickly soaked through with blood. She wrapped a second one around it. He went back to the workshop for a while, but his hand was still bleeding through the cloth, and he stained each reed that he touched. Finally he gave up.

The next day, his hand was red and sore. He couldn't hold anything, and he couldn't work. When he wasn't working, he would usually play the concertina, but he couldn't do that, either. It was strange for his family to see him idle and silent. They never knew, until then, how quiet he was without his music. A few days went by. Every time the bandage was changed, the hand was more swollen, until the skin was so stretched that he couldn't move his fingers.

Then came the morning he had a fever and couldn't get out of bed. Gioseff went for the doctor, but there was nothing he could do. Papa DeMarco tossed and turned in his bed. The sheets, the only set, were soaked with his sweat. He talked to himself and sometimes cried out, but no one could understand him. It was like he was caught in a nightmare and couldn't escape. A day went by like this. And then he gave up words altogether, and for one more day the only sound he made came from his struggle to breathe. He died the next afternoon.

Gioseff took the last reeds his father ever made to the factory, and they bought them. The owner, Signor Zacardelli, said they were sorry for the family, and paid a little extra—*per il funerale* (for the funeral)—"I don't remember how much." Signor Zacardelli said the reeds were good as always. He told Gioseff that his father had been *un bravo artigiano* (a good artist), and he was proud to be able to use them.

I swallowed the lump in my throat while Gioseff sighed and wiped his eyes with the back of his hands. He studied the carpet for a moment, took a deep breath, and picked up his story. When he spoke again, I could feel the weight of it in the room, bearing down on him.

"No two accordions are alike; you know that, right, Mariangela? Signor Zacardelli told me that each one bears the mark of many makers. Most accordions have more than one pair of hands work on them. But somewhere…"

Gioseff broke off again. His hands were trembling and his face was flushed. He struggled to finish what he was saying.

"…*in qualche posto* (somewhere)."

A deep breath.

"Somewhere there is an accordion with my father's last mark inside."

Gioseff was exhausted. He rubbed his forehead and stared at the floor. "I think you should go home now. Take the dollar back to your mother. No lesson today."

I stood up, but I wasn't sure about going. I had never thought about him being lonely before—about what it might be like to have no family, to live in a room in a house full of people, and have nobody at all who understood where you were from. What you had really come from. I just stood there.

"I'll tell you the rest next week," he said quietly.

I took back the dollar he held out to me. He got up and helped me to the hall with my case. He left me at the top of the stairs and silently went into his room.

As I lugged the case down Mrs. Secco's staircase, I heard Gioseff rustling around in his room, looking for something. And then I heard a different accordion. I was sure it wasn't the bright, orchestral Scandalli but something older. And the song it made was sweet and simple, quick and sad—a dance of minor chords.

I stopped there, halfway down. I set my case in front of me, sat down on the step above, and held on tight to the handle. And I just listened, without thinking anything, until the song was over and from Gioseff's room came nothing at all.

CHAPTER 15

Gioseff

I KEPT THE DOLLAR for next week. My mother never noticed. By now, nobody asked what I'd learned after my lesson, but I still had to practice. If I didn't practice, my father wouldn't speak to me at dinner. One night, I got so frustrated with "Old Smoky" that I flung my music stand at the wall. A prong stuck into the plaster and hung there, suspended, before crashing to the bedroom floor. As I stared at the hole in the wall, terrified of what Mamma and Papa would say, I could feel my father's presence in the hall.

I didn't look out and he didn't step in, but I heard him cough gently and say, "Never mind. Just keep practicing," and then he went downstairs.

A few days later, a framed picture I'd never seen before, of a girl in a ballerina costume, mysteriously appeared on the wall, over the hole I'd made in the plaster. Everyone, even Emelina, acted like it had been there all the time.

Curiousity burned through me the whole week, until once again I was sitting in Mrs. Secco's parlor and Gioseff continued his tale.

Gioseff and his brother Guillermo came to Canada the year after their father died. Their mother went back to her village in the mountains to take care of her mother and father. Their grandfather gave the brothers the money for the *viaggio*. From where the money came, the boys never learned.

They shared a bunk in the barracks of steerage. Gioseff had with him a rucksack, a change of clothes, his cap, a Bible, and his father's concertina. Guillermo had his father's tools, even the reed-splicing knife.

Sometimes there were parties down below, and dancing. Gioseff played the concertina.

Another man had a mandolin. There were a couple of other guys with harmonicas. And everybody sang. It was like a dance hall—hot and loud and smoky. The days dragged, but the nights whirled by. Men and women would get up on tables, clap their hands, and bounce their babies on their hips. Sleep? Forget about it.

There wasn't much to do in the daytime, except be sick. Guillermo had his sea legs, but Gioseff was sick in the Bay of Biscay, when the waves got so rough that the whole ship rocked from side to side, like they were locked in the belly of a sick giant. Sometimes Gioseff would go outside and hang onto the ropes to walk, but never with the concertina. The damp sea air and the water that flung itself on deck was bad for the bellows—his father had always said that damp was *la rovina* (the end) to an accordion. Damp bellows would soon stink with mold. Holes would spread in the pleats and sop up the air meant for the reeds. And in no time, all you'd have left was this wheezing wind strainer that was ruined for music.

A few days before they saw land, the night merriments ended. A baby had taken ill and died. Gioseff never saw the baby, and all he remembered of the mother was a woman crying, inconsolable, under a heap of bedclothes. Her bunk was far away from Guillermo and him, but her sorrow filled the whole of steerage. That afternoon, women covered their heads; they wailed and mourned, and their rosary beads swung with the ship as it rode the swells. Others spoke in hushed tones and avoided looking in the direction of the mother. It was very tense; everyone lay in their beds that night, pretending to sleep. Mothers tried to quiet their restless children, out of sympathy, as if to hear their little voices would only make the woman's grief worse.

In the dark, Gioseff took out his concertina and held it for a long time. He played his father's song—the song he'd played at his funeral. When he finished, he felt scared. Maybe it was wrong, what he'd done. But then he heard a sad, gentle voice from across the great room: "*Ancora una volta per piacere* (Again, please, one more time)." And so he played it through again; and when he finished, the voice called for the song again. Gioseff did as he was asked, playing the song over and over again until the voice stopped asking and everyone had fallen asleep.

They made the crossing from Naples to America in eight days. When they stepped off the boat, different languages blurred together in the jostling crowds. Quarantine at Ellis Island was two more days, then they were on a train to Montreal.

In English, the brothers only knew "Good morning" and "Good evening." And even *those* they mixed up. They had to go to a place where they could understand at least some of the people. They weren't used to big cities; their village was just a few hundred people. In Montreal, they didn't know where to begin. Guillermo had heard that there were *calabresi* in British Columbia, and that men made good money in the coal mines. Someone told him about Fernie. There were lots of Italians there—everyone had a job, a house, a vegetable garden. But they didn't have enough money for the fare.

The next morning, Gioseff went out to the front of the station, put his cap down, took the concertina out of his rucksack, and started to play.

They had the money in a week.

He played on the train, mostly to pass the time. People asked him if he knew songs they'd hum. Sometimes he did. Sometimes he could pick up by ear what they were humming. Nobody gave them money in the car where they sat; nobody had any to give. Instead, women unwrapped cloths and took out baskets. So they were never hungry the whole trip. Men offered cigarettes; Guillermo liked those. A few times, when the train stopped, Gioseff would get out, put his cap down for an hour, and play for pennies.

When the train stopped at Winnipeg, Guillermo went to buy food from the concession, and Gioseff stayed out on the platform and played. A man hung around through every song, until the train was nearly ready to leave. He was short, and looked to be bald under his bowler hat. Round as a tomato with a red face to match, he wore a snappy pinstriped suit, with a flower in his buttonhole, and shoes so shiny you could see your face in the toes. He asked if Gioseff wanted to join his vaudeville act. Gioseff didn't understand what he was saying, and just shook his head at him. He went away, but then came hurrying back with someone to translate.

"Two dollars! I give you two dollars a show! Two-fifty! Okay, three! Three is good money! Three dollars a show. What kid makes that kinda money?"

Guillermo came back with a stack of sandwiches in his hands. He looked worried. Gioseff was small for his age, a real *skinnamarink*.

Guillermo was the big one. He was a natural pro-
tector. That was his way, to always look out for his
little brother. It was strange to the brothers that,
in Canada, Gioseff was the one who could put his
cap down and earn enough for both to eat for
another day. Maybe that was hard on his brother.
He was proud, but he was practical, too. In a way,
the accordion always separated them. When
Guillermo was five, he refused to learn it. He
would ball his hands into tight fists whenever their
father tried to show him which buttons to press.

Gioseff just shook his head at the man with the
tomato-face and said no. Finally, the man gave up,
tossed a folded dollar bill in Gioseff's cap, winked,
and said, "Good luck, kiddo. I hope what you're
going to is worth what you're giving up."

On the train, Gioseff unfolded the dollar. It
was real, and whole, and inside was a card:
Bartholomew Dickens McKenzie, Vaudeville
Impresario—a little girl sitting across the aisle
read it out loud. The card went spinning out the

window as the train pulled out of the station. When Gioseff got to Fernie, all he planned to do was to go to school.

They had left Italy at the end of the summer; it was mid-September by the time they arrived. Fernie was far enough for the brothers. The town was much bigger than their village in Italy, and the buildings newer. But the color! Everything was so green...the mountains around them. Guillermo and Gioseff were used to a brown and dusty village, where trees were spindly and sparse, and goats ate the grass faster than it could grow.

It was only later they noticed the coal dust that settled on everything. It covered the grass and the gardens. When it was windy, it would blow into laundry hung out to dry. And then you could hear women all over town, shouting and crying about having to do washday all over again.

Guillermo got work almost right away, and their landlady, Signora Brisario, enrolled Gioseff in school. She was a nice lady. She had five kids of her own, and no husband. He'd been a coal miner and was killed one day in a cave-in at one of the Coal Creek mines.

They put Gioseff in the third grade. In Italy, he'd had an eighth-grade education. But because he couldn't speak English, in Canada it was back to grade three. The teacher didn't seem to know what to do with him. One of the little Italian kids told Gioseff that if he spoke Italian in class, the teacher would make him wear a bell around his neck for a week. So he never spoke at all. Sometimes, Signora Brisario packed with his lunch a little soda bottle filled with red wine and a cork in the top, like back home. A few of the other Italian kids had the same. Some drank it; some poured it out. Others gave it to the tougher, older boys—not Italians, but kids with English names, the kids who'd pin them against a wall at recess, rob them, and then sneak off to the woods to drink.

Mostly everybody left Gioseff alone. He just didn't fit in. Too old for his class and too big to get mugged for his wine. The kids his own age thought he was too stupid to bother with because he didn't speak English. And, if that wasn't all of it, word got around that Guillermo was Gioseff's brother. People liked Guillermo— he was strong and hardworking and brave. It didn't matter that he didn't speak English; the men on his crew spoke mostly Italian. He volunteered to be on the mine's rescue team, and spent Saturdays and Sundays doing push-ups and running. He joined the soccer team in the spring. He was the youngest but one of the best on the team, like he'd been in Italy.

After school, Gioseff would head to the mine and work for an hour or two at the picking table, sorting coal from junk rock. There were a couple of other kids doing the work, a few old men who didn't go below anymore, and a few guys who'd been hurt on the job or in the war.

Gioseff learned a little English working at the table, but not fast enough. At school, he felt like an idiot. It was boring to sit there all day and not get anything that was going on. He tried practicing fingerings, sometimes on his desk; but the teacher thought he was trying to be annoying and rapped his fingers with a ruler. He kept doing it—it kept him from going crazy—but on his knees, where she couldn't see.

He stuck it out at school for a year. By May, he had grown so much that he couldn't squeeze his knees under the desk. He sat on a stool in the back of the room. By then Gioseff could speak a little English, even read some, but he hadn't learned it in the classroom. In June, when it seemed the black underground shafts of the mine would offer more freedom than the classroom, he left and never went back. The Signora didn't approve. The morning that he started work, she handed him his lunch pail and said grimly, "I hope what you're going to is worth what you're giving up."

That first year, the concertina was stuffed in the back of the closet that Guillermo and Gioseff shared. He didn't play it much. He didn't want the coal dust that stained his fingers after a shift at the picking table to ruin the one thing he had of his father's.

But after Guillermo got Gioseff the job underground, he took the concertina out. He smudged it some, but he said it was better than not playing at all. Sometimes the days were so short that Gioseff would leave the surface before dawn, work all day in the dark and damp, and come up into darkness. In the winter, he forgot the sun ever rose at all. He said he needed the light that the music made. He missed his parents and his friends. He missed long summers, dry heat, siestas in the sun, and the smell of afternoons. But he got used to it.

One year, he told himself. One year in the mines, to teach himself English, and then he'd find some other work.

He lasted nine.

The brothers grew up. Guillermo got married. Gioseff played at his wedding—he was so proud! He and his wife bought a little house nearby. Gioseff could've gone with him, but he figured that pretty soon there wouldn't be room, so he stayed at Signora Brisario's. Guillermo became captain of the soccer team and captain of his shift's rescue crew. They'd compete with rescue teams from other mines in relay races and tests of strength and speed. Year after year, Guillermo's team was unbeatable.

Gioseff had a girlfriend, Maria. She was a chambermaid in one of the hotels. They'd go to dances and house parties on Saturday nights. Gioseff usually played his concertina. There were other guys who played the accordion— Carl, Al, and Joe. Carl was from Germany; he taught Gioseff how to play his "piano with suspenders." It had 120 bass buttons and 41 keys— a Goliath next to Gioseff's little concertina.

Al could read sheet music. He'd ride up to the dances with his accordion case balanced between the handlebars of his bicycle. His girl-friend had to run alongside to keep up with him. Joe was the real performer. Loved getting up for a crowd. He knew any song anybody'd holler out: folksongs, big band, blues, even. And he could play anything on his beautiful black accordion—an Italo-American all the way from Chicago. It was something else. Joe was a coal miner, too, but you'd never know it from his keyboard; it was spotless. Before he played, he'd always polish it up first.

After his kids were born, Guillermo couldn't send so much money home to Italy. Gioseff was earning plenty more than he needed, so he sent some to their mother, and put some by every payday for a piano accordion. He found the Scandalli in a pawnshop in Nelson. Three dollars a week. It took him almost a year to buy it.

He didn't think much about the mine being

dangerous. Well, not all the time. It was something they all knew, but Gioseff didn't begin each day thinking, *I hope I make it out today*. A couple of times there were bumps in the shaft where he worked. The whole tunnel would move; loose rock would fall free. He remembered falling down once. And he got bruised by rock fall. That scared him—the other guys on the shift, too. They took the cage up early that day, but everyone went back in again, the next morning.

As he got older, he hardened up to it. Learned to think of other things, like keeping warm. You felt the cold, fast, if you stopped moving. It took concentration to work in the narrow light of a headlamp and lantern. Only in the moment that the tunnel heaved would he panic and think, *O mio Dio, quest'è la fine!* (Oh my God, this is the end!) Then, as everything settled, he'd get calm again. It wasn't his day to die.

But Gioseff was nervous the day they sent him and a couple other guys down to timber up a weak spot where the rock was bad—loose all over, with pieces crumbling off. You could hear them from farther down the tunnel, as if a phantom miner were at work. They were supposed to build a few more pit props, to support the walls and ceiling. Gioseff liked construction work, and welcomed the break from mining.

The crew put up some beams, and quit for lunch around noon. Gioseff had just finished a sandwich, and he still had his gloves off when they felt it coming. The tunnel quaked, and rock rained free. Boulders knocked Gioseff down, pinned his arms and legs in a trap, and squeezed the wind out of his lungs. He could feel rock against his bones. In seconds, he was locked inside a tomb of rubble.

In the aftermath, he listened to dust and grit and stones fall, but he couldn't hear any voices. One man had been killed immediately—crushed to death by the rock fall. Another had been knocked unconscious and was badly bruised, but he pulled through all in one piece. At first, Gioseff tried to call out. It was like the kind of nightmare where you're straining so hard to scream that you don't make any sound at all. There was blood mixed with chips of rock in his mouth. He spat it out, and more bled in. He thought maybe he'd faint—he wished for that. His hard hat was gone. He had no light. Fear and thick coal dust made him weep. His eyes stung with grit and tears, and, whether they were opened or closed, all he could see was black. He could move his eyelids, toes, and right arm. Maybe he was only bruised. But his left arm burned with pain, and he couldn't feel his left hand.

When you stop moving in the mine, said Gioseff, you feel the cold. Very quickly Gioseff was freezing. His teeth chattered, and the grit in his mouth made him vomit. He had to spit it out to keep from choking.

And then the cold didn't seem quite so bad. He thought if he dreamed of his village in the summer, that was all he would need to stay warm. Delirious, he told himself, "Keep your face to the sun." And he was sure he could feel it—the sun on his face—and, if he kept still, so would the sky; no clouds would move and he would still have his sun.

He fell unconscious. Hours went by and he slipped in and out of dreams and darkness. He could hear voices, but couldn't stay awake.

Then he heard Guillermo. There were others, too, but he could only recognize Guillermo's voice. They lifted the weight off his legs and arms, but he couldn't feel anything and didn't move.

Guillermo told Gioseff afterward that they'd worked with picks and shovels to get to him, and they lifted the last rocks with their bare hands. Gioseff's left arm was broken, and they couldn't see his hand; it was crushed under a rock and covered in debris. But they had him almost free. Gioseff woke up to see Guillermo, his mask off, bending over him. He was crying. His face was black with coal dust, and so were his tears.

In the lantern light, Gioseff could see a little blade in Guillermo's hand—their father's knife. Guillermo looked down at Gioseff's arm. Gioseff turned his head and saw that only three of his fingers were free. He couldn't see the other two—they were sealed under the rock.

"There's just the skin left connecting you, that's all," Guillermo said to Gioseff. The struggle to steady his voice made him sound old. "We can't move the rock. I have to cut the skin to free you."

"Do it! Do it!" Gioseff said to him. He felt crazy with panic. He was so close to freedom. But Guillermo didn't move.

"*Per piacere, fratello, per piacere!* (Please, brother, please!)" Gioseff begged and turned his head away. He didn't feel the cuts, but he heard Guillermo retch beside him and knew it was done. They lifted Gioseff onto a stretcher. He looked for Guillermo, but all he could see were bands of light from headlamps, crossing each other, parting, crossing back. And then he sank away from them, into darkness.

"They think I don't remember it," said Gioseff. "Guillermo thinks I don't remember it. I do; it's only that I have never wanted him to know. It was worse for him—to cut the hand of his only brother, the one who makes the father's music. I think that is a thousand times worse."

CHAPTER 16

The Same, Only Different

GIOSEFF WAS IN THE HOSPITAL a couple of days. He slept a lot in the daytime, and lay awake at night. When everybody else was sleeping, he'd lie there and listen to the bats, one floor above, fly in and out of the hospital attic. It was the same soft rustling sound he heard in his room at the Signora's. He found it peaceful.

"The bones of a bat's wings are really its hands, Mariangela," said Gioseff. "Did you know that? Thinner than a toothpick. Their whole lives depend on their wings. What is a bat that can't fly? Wing skin can tear, small breaks may heal; but if the bone breaks clean off, there's no growing back. No balance between the wings— no way of staying aloft."

Gioseff found a bat once, clinging to the side

of a freshly tarred building. It had died there, unable to free itself.

His left arm was in a cast; the hand wrapped in bandages that a nurse changed every day. The pain in his arm swelled and pulsed through his hand. They gave him morphine in the first week, which helped some. But there were long hours where the pain burned through. It made him confused.

Guillermo visited every day, after his shift. He told the doctors what had happened to their father—the knife cut, the infection that killed him. He refused to take Gioseff home. So they kept him in longer, until the danger had passed.

After he was released, he changed his own bandages. He made himself stare at the two little stumps, where his fingers had been. He didn't work, and he couldn't play either of his accordions. Although his right hand was okay, he'd lost the strength to pull the bellows with the left.

He read a lot. His English was still pretty poor. He would read out loud, whole sentences of words he didn't understand—*Robinson Crusoe, Treasure Island, Lorna Doone*... At first, he read purely to escape his own thoughts. But then, gradually, meaning began to seep through.

After about six weeks, the bandages came off for the last time. Gioseff went back to the picking table. The work seemed particularly bleak. He was no longer a miner; his place was now with the cripples and the old men. He worked with his right hand and kept his left tucked inside a pocket. If he'd been any older, you'd have thought he was a casualty of the Great War.

He stopped going to the house parties and dances. Maria visited him in the hospital every day. He didn't talk to anyone much, not even her. Bitterness made him quiet; he could feel it seeping through his skin. Maria felt it, too. After he'd been home for a while, she stopped coming around. But, from his bench at the picking table, he still saw Joe, coming and going on his shift. He'd stop by and ask how Gioseff was doing. And Gioseff couldn't talk, not even to Joe; hard to look him in the eye. It was the same with Guillermo.

Most of the summer was lost this way. One Saturday night, Joe pedaled around to the house to see Gioseff. He started to talk about the accordion. He said he'd take it back to the pawn shop, if that's what Gioseff wanted.

"You know what, though?" he asked.

"What?" Gioseff said sourly. He wished he'd just go away.

"A real miner'd find a way to play it."

"I'm not a miner."

"Not anymore, you're not. But nine years underground has given you enough of a miner's heart to pull out of this. Nobody is ever one thing in life. You were a miner, and you'll go on to other things you can't even imagine yet. And you can go through your life with your music, or you can go it alone. For me, I'd rather have an accordion over my shoulder than no friend at all. When you need her, she'll always come to your rescue."

Then he opened the case of Gioseff's Scandalli and lifted it onto his knees. He folded his left baby finger and ring finger in against his palm. He played the bass buttons with the three he held free. A real quick piece—"Sharpshooter's March." He had to work those fingers twice as fast to compensate. But you'd never know from the music. When he finished, he handed the accordion over to Gioseff.

"You leave it too long, you'll never get it all back." He clapped Gioseff on the shoulder and stood up. "C'mon, kid. You play better than anyone in this town. Don't let it go in the can."

He left before Gioseff could try to argue. Coming from anyone else, it would've sounded like a mother's praise. But if Joe said it, then you had something to believe.

"Mariangela, do you know what gave me the most trouble at first? Not the lazy fingers I had left, but the two I'd lost. I kept thinking they were there, on their buttons. I couldn't get why the chords didn't come out. You think it's all your mind that learns an instrument? The body has a memory, too. And it takes over, where the thinking stops and real music begins.

"My phantom fingers," said Gioseff, stretching out his hands. "I still feel them trying to get in on the fastest pieces.

"When I left for Vancouver, nobody told me, 'I hope what you're going to is better than what you're leaving behind.' So I said it to myself. On the train, I thought about a miner's heart. How you're not born with it. It's one of the few things that grows in the dark.

"Mafia?" Gioseff snorted. "No Mafia. You could tell that Lister kid the truth. But he wouldn't get it, would he? Let him think what he likes—serves him right, to be just a little afraid."

Gioseff laughed then and asked me what I wanted to hear today. I'd known since the week before.

"Play me your father's song."

He looked surprised.

"Okay," he said gruffly, flexed his left hand and picked up his accordion with the right.

"That I can do."

CHAPTER 17

For Everyone to Hear

THE NEXT TUESDAY was dry and clear. The air felt more like spring than winter as Dot, Esther, and I walked home from school. Sonia was running a block ahead of us. When we got to my house, Gioseff was just climbing the stairs to the door. Dot stopped in her tracks to stare at him Esther slowed down.

"He's so handsome!" Dot cooed under her breath.

I was embarrassed to see Gioseff there, but relieved, too. Maybe he was canceling the lesson. At least I wouldn't have to go by Dennis's house alone today. I wished there were another way to get to Mrs. Secco's, but it was all lanes around the back of the street, and I needed the pavement to pull the wagon.

"Hi, Mariangela!" said Gioseff, hopping down the stairs. "Let's do a different kind of lesson today—you don't need your accordion. We're going to Stefani's store. We need a little inspiration!"

Dot nudged me from behind and Esther started coughing, loudly.

"Gioseff, these are my friends, Dot and Esther. Dot and Esther, this is Gioseff."

Dot bounded forward a few steps with a cheery "Hiya!" Esther just shifted on her feet beside me, studied her shoes, and fiddled with the hem of her skirt. She looked like she needed to go to the bathroom. Badly.

"Can we come with you?" piped up Dot. "I have a nickel. We could get a Sweet Marie!"

Gioseff said sure. So we dropped our schoolbags on the front porch and followed him down the street, the block and a half, to Stefani's *Generi Alimentari*. Mr. Stefani's daughter, Sabina, was behind the counter. Sabina was very pretty—slim and blonde like my mother, with a long, flat nose and big, brown eyes so dark that you could mistake them for black. She had just finished high school the year before, and now worked in her father's store.

For a second or two, Gioseff forgot all about us. He lingered in front of Sabina's counter and made small talk about the royal visit. He asked Sabina if she thought she'd be able to go, and she said no, they'd be open the whole day. And since her mother had died, her father had no one else to be in the store. Gioseff seemed sort of nervous talking to Sabina, putting his hands in his pockets and taking them out about a dozen times. He said it was too bad that she wouldn't get to see the king and queen. And Sabina's pale face went pink, all the way down to the neckline of her dress.

Dot cut in to buy her chocolate bar, which she shared with us, although I noticed she didn't offer any to Gioseff, who kept talking to Sabina. The way he looked at her was kind of nice, in a sappy way. I didn't know what any of it had to do with my accordion lesson. And I didn't care.

Then Mr. Stefani came out from the back. "Gioseff, *come stai*? (how are you?)" He held out his hands in exclamation, then said hello to all of us by name. Mr. Stefani was a very tiny man. He was about my height, with just a fringe of gray hair around his head, like a monk. He always wore spectacles and spotless white aprons that were too long in the front.

Uncle Tony said that Signor Stefani had a heart as big as a house, but he must be the poorest shopkeeper in the whole East End. He was always getting broken into. Uncle Tony would have to go, in the middle of the night, to change the locks. Most of the time, Uncle Tony said that the thieves didn't even bother prying open the cash register; they were hungry and all they stole was food. Even so, going by on the way to school, we'd often see him handing out loaves of bread to sad-faced, skinny men in dirty clothes.

And Sabina put out saucers of milk for the neighborhood cats. Once, when she stepped back inside, we saw a hobo come furtively round the corner and drink the saucer dry.

"Wha' can I do fo' you an' all-a dees pretty girls?" Mr. Stefani asked Gioseff.

Gioseff said we'd come to hear a little music, and he asked if he could see Mr. Stefani's record collection. Mr. Stefani led him to the back of the store and Gioseff came back, a minute or two later, with a record tucked under his arm.

Mr. Stefani went over to the record player that was tucked in a crowded corner of the shop, and Gioseff motioned for us to follow him outside. We stood there for a moment in silence. And then, from over our heads, came the sound of an accordion, beginning a song. It came from the speakers wired to the outside corner of the store. Sometimes in the summer, Mr. Stefani played music in the evenings and on Saturday mornings, for everyone in the neighborhood who didn't have a gramophone.

"'Drink to Me Only with Thine Eyes,'" said Gioseff, and, as he peered into the shop window to see what Sabina was doing, he continued. "That's the name of the song. That's what you're going to learn for Flavia Antonelli's wedding."

I was aghast. Who had told him about Flavia's wedding?

"I can't play that! I can't even get 'On Top of Old Smoky'!" How am I going to learn that in a couple of weeks?"

"It's really not that difficult a song. No sharps, no flats, not a single black key to worry about. Listen, there's the melody. Just listen to it and follow along with your fingers, as if you were playing it yourself," Gioseff demonstrated, tapping his right fingers on his knee, as if there were a keyboard on his pant leg. "See? Many of the notes are the same, and they're mostly quarter notes. You play them every day when you practice your scales."

"Besides, it's a wedding! Everybody'll be happy. They'll be with you—you'll see. It'll sound good to them no matter how you play it. You'll know by all the tapping feet. They're with you; you have them, they're in the music. Don't worry about it."

I sat on the bench and leaned against the store window. Gioseff popped his head inside the door and asked Mr. Stefani to start the record again. This time I listened hard. Not to my thoughts, for once, but to the music.

I closed my eyes. I imagined it was summer, and we all had ice cream, except Gioseff was holding mine. And I was actually playing the piece. And Mr. Stefani's shop was full of customers. And they were all clapping. And people were waltzing in the street; I could hear their shoes softly scuff the pavement.

And then I opened my eyes and saw it was true, at least part of it was. Dot and Esther were laughing and dancing around, and an old, wrinkled couple had joined them. And even though they were dancing in heavy winter coats, their waltz steps were small and perfect and graceful. Mr. Stefani was standing in the window, conducting the air, and Sabina had come outside to stand very close beside Gioseff. He had both his hands up in the air now, as if he were playing the song himself for everyone to hear. And it was easy, just by looking at him, to believe that he was.

CHAPTER 18

Maybe Just One

AFTER WE'D LISTENED to the whole record, it was almost dark. Dot and Esther were going to be late for dinner, so they yelled out good-byes and ran ahead of us. Gioseff walked me back to my house. He didn't say much, and I couldn't think of anything really important, so I just said that Sabina was nice, and it was too bad about her mother. And he said something about how he knew what that felt like, only for him it was his father.

He said that when he came to Vancouver, Mr. Stefani had given him his first sign-painting job. Every day, he worked out behind the shop and Mr. Stefani played records, or radio operas, over the loudspeakers. I told him Mr Stefani had the nicest sign in the neighborhood, with a fancy, swirled capital *S* and *A*, for Stefani's Alimentari.

"'Drink to Me' is in your music book," he said to me, hurrying the subject back to music, when we got to the bottom of my steps.

"There's not a lot of time to practice, if you want to be good and ready for the wedding. Give your Mamma back today's dollar. Maybe we'll have an extra lesson in a week or two. You got any homework tonight?"

"Not much."

"Then, you think you could get started and try out the fingerings?"

Somewhere on the walk home I had begun to think that maybe, just maybe, I could learn one song. I still didn't have the bass buttons of my left hand down for "Old Smoky," but I could recognize the melody when I played. Besides, I didn't particularly like "Old Smoky"—too cowboyish, corny. But "Drink to Me Only" was pretty, in a classical kind of way. Something you'd play on a real instrument. Like a piano.

I promised Gioseff I'd try, and headed up the

stairs. For a second I wondered if I should ask him in for dinner; Mamma was always saying I should bring him back to eat with us after my lesson. I just about turned around to ask, but then, through the front door, I could hear Mamma's voice from the living room, all trembly and tense. She was arguing in Italian with Mr. Zucchi, who sometimes gave her department-store orders for children's clothes.

"I already told you no! I only sew girls' clothes. Never for boys. I told you before! Why ask me again?"

I slipped inside and closed the door carefully, so as to make no sound. Without removing my coat, I tiptoed over to the stairs and sat down. Mamma had always been firm about this strange, mysterious rule that she would never sew for boys. She made my father's work shirts and pants; that was all. Everyone in the neighborhood knew you could not commission a little pair of trousers or a small blue shirt from her.

"*Bambina, bambino, bambini,*" said Mr. Zucchi hotly. "What's the difference? Little boys' clothes? Little girls'? You sew the same. This is a big order! I'll pay you extra!"

That had to take a lot for Mr. Zucchi to promise. Papa said he was a terrible cheapskate, a real *Pidocchioso*. A cheaparoni.

It's amazing, the secrets that come out when people are fighting. For a moment, I thought Mamma would tell Mr. Zucchi why not, and then I'd understand, too. But all she said was, "*Dio me liberi* (God help me), I...said...NO. No is what I mean!" Mamma's eyes were flashing and looked about to burst with tears. She stamped her foot angrily, and her heel made a sharp cracking sound on the hardwood floor.

Mr. Zucchi slammed his case closed and said that, if she wouldn't do the order, then he had nothing for her that week. Then he turned to leave, so I scrambled backward up the stairs.

"*Va bene cosi!* (Fine!)" said Mamma sharply

as Mr. Zucchi grabbed his coat and strode indignantly out the door.

"Maybe not the next week, either! Or the week after that," said Mr. Zucchi, testing Mamma with a warning. She didn't seem to care.

"*Va bene!*" she called after him down the dark city street. "*Faccio una vacanza!* (I'll take a holiday!)"

Of course, she wouldn't go anywhere. My parents never went anywhere; they crossed half the world to come to Canada, and that was far enough for both of them.

So Mamma went to bed instead.

CHAPTER 19

A Secret Curse

OF COURSE, BECAUSE SHE WAS MAMMA, she didn't go to bed right away. She cooked dinner silently, and, as we ate, refused to sit down. After Sonia and I had washed the dishes, Mamma handed me a soft ball of semolina dough for ravioli. While she chopped vegetables into tiny cubes for soup, I rolled and cut out the squares, put spinach filling in the middle of each, and sealed them closed. We didn't speak but listened to Sonia chattering away as she clipped the latest news of the royal visit. The paper said that the king and queen would almost surely bring their crowns to Canada. If they did, it would be the first time the crown jewels had crossed the Atlantic.

"Spiffy!" cried Sonia. "It says the queen will be wearing a platinum crown, set entirely with diamonds! Her crown has a diamond called the Koh-i-noor in it, which she can take out of the crown and wear pinned to her dress.

"Ooooh," cooed Sonia as she read ahead. "Listen to this. It says there's a superstition surrounding the stone: it can only be worn by women for fear of an ancient curse!" Sonia read the rest of the story, earnestly looking for what the curse might be, but there was no mention of it. Instead, the reporter went on to describe the great secrecy surrounding the queen's dresses for the trip. She was to take fifty gowns and coats, several furs, and a different hat for each day's ensemble. But no one would know the designs until the queen actually stepped out in them.

I thought Mamma would be interested in this, but she didn't seem to be listening. Nor did she come upstairs to tuck us in that night. In bed, I listened to her sounds coming from the kitchen. I could see in my mind's eye how she rubbed olive oil, rosemary, and oregano into the chicken before roasting it; how she pounded veal chops until they were as thin as a slice of pancetta bacon; and how she stirred the sauce to keep it from burning. I drifted off to sleep, and when I awoke, before dawn, I tiptoed down the stairs to see Mamma scrubbing the kitchen floor. Her hair was wildly askew. Her eyes were bloodshot and her face was red and wet with perspiration. I slipped back up to bed and lay there. Fear made me quiet.

When we came down for breakfast, a week's worth of food was cooling on the counter. Mamma handed me her crumpled apron, pushed back the damp hair in her eyes, and said, "Mariangela, you take care of your sisters and your father. I'm going to bed now.

"And, Mariangela?"

"*Yes*, Mamma?"

"Don't forget to practice."

CHAPTER 20
Coraggio

MOTHERS! barked the ad in the newspaper, right next to Dorothy Dix's column. *Feed your nervous children Marmite!*

Marmite was the stuff Dot sometimes had in her lettuce sandwiches. To me it smelled like burnt soup. Dot loved it. She said she had egg on toast with Marmite every Saturday for lunch, and it was her favorite. Once, I asked Mamma if she'd buy us a jar, but she just laughed and called it crazy English food. She was right, too. Marmite smelled so bad, I was afraid to try a bite. Esther said it smelled like cat vomit, which she was an expert in because their cluttered house hid an uncountable number of strays. But the word *nervous* in the advertisement got me thinking. Dot was never nervous. She talked to boys and climbed trees. She stuck up her hand in class and never cared if she got an answer wrong. What if Marmite were some miracle food? And what if I ate enough of it before Flavia's wedding? Maybe I could play without being afraid.

I couldn't ask Mamma, since Papa said she was having a rest. We were under strict orders not to bother her. Sometimes I saw her shuffle to the bathroom, stand there, and brush out her long hair. She hadn't put it back in braids since the morning she took to her bed. While the rest of us tiptoed around Mamma's holiday, Emelina took it differently. She curled up with Billydog, in the crook of Mamma's arm, each afternoon at naptime. And she slept, drooling on the sleeve of Mamma's nightgown.

I was beginning to feel desperate. Flavia's wedding was two weeks away, and I still couldn't get the bass button accompaniment to my song. It would be like Gigi picking out a song on the piano with only her right hand. Baby stuff. Everybody would know I couldn't really play.

The next day, I asked Dot if she could bring me a jar of Marmite from home.

"Whaddya wan' it for?"

"It says in the paper nervous children should eat Marmite."

"Really? It says that? You nervous about something?"

"Playing accordion at Flavia's wedding."

"Say no more. I'll bring it back after lunch," said Dot. Even my best friend thought I had something to be nervous about.

Dot's schoolbag was bulging as she trudged home with Esther and me from school that day. She'd brought an almost-full jar of Marmite back after lunch, with a few slices of bread and some lettuce wrapped in wax paper. Nonna was in the kitchen getting Emelina to hold the dustpan while she swept. We hurried upstairs to my bedroom without taking our coats off, and I lifted up the window. Then we climbed out onto the roof of the cowshed, which was where we went when Dot had an Oh Henry! bar to share and we were hiding from Sonia and Emelina.

"Did'ja bring your knife?"

Esther took out a pocketknife her dad had found and handed it to Dot. "I don't want any," she said, not meeting our eyes. Esther'd been pretty quiet for the last couple of weeks, but when we asked what was eating her, she wouldn't say.

She actually looked hungry, but then, she always looked that way. Esther's family ate okay, but not food Mamma would ever let us touch. Always day-old or seconds. Or the bags of lumpy vegetables the grocer said were only fit for hobos.

The lettuce was crushed and wilted from banging around in Dot's bag, and the bread was squished. But Dot hacked at it anyway and fixed us some sandwiches. For herself, she spread

Marmite as thin as a smudge of eyelashes on a piece of bread. But for me, she scooped out a thick, brown dollop and mashed it down.

"*Coraggio*! (Courage!)" I said, and took a bite.

Esther was right; it tasted awful. I gagged and spat it over the roof of the cowshed. "How can you eat that stuff?" I wailed at Dot. She just laughed.

"Nothin' like it!" said Dot, with her mouth full. "Mmm! Tastes like more!" and she took another gigantic bite.

I threw my sandwich in the alley and realized immediately that it meant confession to Father Paul and a whole bunch of Hail Marys.

"Can I tell you something?" asked Esther in a glum voice.

"Sure," said Dot with her mouth full. "You sure you don't want some?" she asked, holding out the sandwich to Esther.

Esther thought about it for a second, reached

out, and took a big bite. *"Coraggio!"* she said doubtfully, and swallowed.

"Go on, Esther. What is it?" I asked, as gently as I could.

"I have cousins in Germany," said Esther, wiping a hand across the back of her mouth. "My parents are really worried about them; they think something bad is going to happen."

"You mean because of what Hitler's doing to the Jews?" We'd all read about it in the papers.

Esther nodded. "And I heard them talking last night. They said they've lost their home."

"Oh, Esther. That's bad."

"I know."

Esther stared down blankly at the alley. Dot held out what was left of her sandwich. "Go on, you have it," she said to Esther. *"Coraggio,"* she repeated softly. *"Coraggio."*

CHAPTER 21

Stump and Willow

WHEN I WAS REALLY SMALL, I thought the Holy Spirit lived in my Uncle Tony's attic. Uncle Tony talked all the time about getting a boarder, but he never did. Sonia and I figured he didn't want to put God out on the street. There had to be better places for God to live than Uncle Tony's, even though they had more money than my parents and an upright piano—*and* cousin Gigi to play it perfectly.

Gigi was sixteen. Tall and slim as a piano key, she had long, thick, black hair that she could wear loose if she wanted, or braided and bowed. How she wore her hair was up to her. Zia Letizia had never told the barber, "Cut it short, I can't afford to come back every week," the way my mother did. And as a result, we—Emelina, Sonia, and I— were all bobbed up around the ears. I saw myself as a stump next to Gigi's willow. Gigi's slim fingers would reach for the high and low keys in graceful sweeps, and her arms floated up and down like a swan opening and closing its wings.

Yes, God would have missed Gigi's playing if He'd had to get another place to live. He'd miss the smells of Nonna's sauce, her *panettone* baking, and her pretty voice singing folk songs while she worked. God, being God, would have sagely steered clear of my accordion racket at our house on Union Street. But I didn't think he was actually at my Uncle Tony's solely because of Gigi's nightly piano performance. Her music was like a bonus. No, the proof I had that God lived in Uncle Tony's attic, and not at the Sacred Heart at Keefer and Campbell, was that my Nonna talked to him there.

Nonna spent her days in the kitchen, except for her little siestas in her room after lunch. And that's where she talked to God. She asked him a lot about housework and cooking. I heard her say, "Too much salt in the sauce? Little more sugar, mebbe?" then she'd look up at the ceiling and nod when she got her answer. She and God were mostly in agreement. There were endless mysteries of laundry for God and my Nonna to ponder together. Nonna sought God's opinion on why there were so many shirts to wash some weeks; what kind of a stain was on Giulietta's blouse; where her dirty socks and underwear were hiding; and how a child who generally avoided clothes could get so many dresses dirty.

Nonna was mostly in Uncle Tony's house, or ours. So I was glad she had God to keep her company. Sometimes she even got angry at her constant companion, and would shake her fist at the ceiling. Except for once, I only ever saw her mad at God about food—things like a scorched sauce or an overdone chicken. "Eet'sa gonna be dry!" And God should've kept a better eye on the cooking when Nonna shuffled out of the kitchen to answer the phone.

God knew Nonna both feared and loved the telephone. She feared it because the caller might not speak Italian, and the conversation would be a brief but shaming ordeal. But she loved it, too, because it was more likely they did speak Italian. Nonna was brave when it came to answering the telephone. She would leave whatever she was doing for the ringing from the alcove down the hall. If the call was in English, there was no risk to the meal, as Nonna would only say to the operator, "You call-a back, please." But if she heard Italian piped through from the other side, all was forgotten. And away she would go, with talk of the house, the family, and the neighborhood.

The sauce then might scorch. The biscotti might harden to rock in the oven. But God never interrupted Nonna on the phone. When at last she hung up and came back to the kitchen, it was often to a whiff of smoke in the air. Nonna would bustle about, stirring and scraping the black bottom of the saucepot, and loudly demand why God hadn't let her know.

The week that Mamma stayed in bed, we went every night to eat at Uncle Tony and Zia Letizia's. The week wore on, and each night Nonna would glance past us as we trooped into the kitchen to kiss her hello. Her face would fall a little further each time, to see that we came again without Mamma. By the end of the week, Nonna was grim and quiet. She cooked, but in a silent, brooding way.

Sunday night, we were all in the dining room around the table, except for Nonna, who would not come out of the kitchen. We could hear her, slamming and dropping things and talking angrily all the while. "Go help your Nonna," Papa said to Sonia and me, and we got up and went to the kitchen.

Nonna's back was turned. She was shaking her fist up at the attic. "Why, God? Why did you take so much from me? I had a good husband. I had a grandson. I had sisters. Now, my daughter? You want my daughter, too?"

Nonna started to cry. She lowered her arm and covered her face with her hands. It made me frightened. This was my Nonna—Nonna, who was not afraid to shake her fist at the Holy Spirit; Nonna, who was never sick, and who never stopped feeding us. My strong Nonna—weeping in the kitchen.

I whispered to Sonia, "You go back. Don't tell Papa." And I could see that Sonia was afraid, too, as she turned to leave. Nonna saw me there and held out her arms.

"Mariangela, you gotta get your Mamma outta da bed," Nonna said, trying to smile, to sound positive, as if it would be easy. She tilted my face back, smoothing my hair behind my ears. "When you go home, you getta her up, you promise me?" Nonna's face was red and wet, and her eyelids hung down, heavy with tears.

"Yes, Nonna," I said, but I must have looked

unsure. My eyebrows always gave me away. They frowned for me even when I didn't mean to; they showed my every doubt.

"Don't try. You do it. You her daughter. She listen to you."

CHAPTER 22

Per i Bambini, Per il Futuro

"Mamma?"

I stood in the doorway of my parents' room and my voice seemed too small to carry to where my mother lay in her bed. I shivered and started to pull the cardigan I was wearing, hers, tightly around me. I heard Mamma's voice inside my head, *Careful. Don't stretch it,* and I quickly clasped my hands behind my back. The curtains were open. The only light in the room came from the streetlamp outside, a thin arc of moon, and a few stars that surrounded it, like moths drawn to the glow.

In the bluish light, Mamma's face, turned toward the window, looked sunken and old. Her hair was unbound and hung limply over her shoulders. It made me ache to look at her.

"Mamma, what happened?"

I waited there in the doorway, on the threshold of Mamma's silence, for a long time. Better to ask for the truth…after all, that was what Mamma had said about Gioseff. But family was different. Uncle Tony once said it wasn't doors or safes or treasure chests—it was family secrets that were the hardest to unlock. And I knew Mamma had something locked inside that was so heavy it made it hard for her to live.

Mamma lay very still on her bed, as if she were using all her energy to make a decision. Finally she took a deep breath and turned to me.

"Come, sit on the bed, Mariangela." Mamma's voice was crystal clear in the cold room. "I'm going to tell you something that happened a long time ago.

"Your father and I were married in Italy; you know that. And when your father decided we would come to Canada, we were already almost a family, because I was going to have a baby.

"I didn't want to come. I had work—I sewed in a factory, and your father was apprenticed to a builder. We were very poor, but everyone was poor. All I could think about was what we had to lose. All your father could dream about was what we had to gain. Your father began to talk to your Uncle Tony about his dream to come to Canada. Tony thought about America, where people locked up riches we couldn't imagine. For a man of his trade, it was the place to be. And very soon after, the idea took hold. Uncle Tony and Zia Letizia had their tickets. The day they left for the ship, your uncle gave an envelope to me. It held enough *lire* for three passages across the sea and for the train to Vancouver— for Nonna, your father, and me.

"It was more money than I had seen in my life. All I could think was, if I had a match, I would burn it. Only the sin of such a thing stopped me. And there was something else—I was going to have a baby. I thought this might change things, but your father was more sure than ever. 'For the children, for the future,' he said to me with great confidence, over and over. And gradually, as I grew larger with the baby, I was able to set my fear to one side.

"Tony wrote to us from Canada. He said he had collected promises from the owners of many construction companies, that they would hire your father as soon as he arrived. And he asked for Nonna to come soon, as Zia Letizia had just given birth to a baby girl, your cousin Gigi.

"I had a boy. A tiny, perfect little boy, with blonde hair and blue eyes. We were overjoyed. We called him Tomaso, after your grandfather. I felt I had everything I could possibly want. I began to doubt and fear the trip to Canada again. I cried and begged to stay in Italy, but by now, Nonna was eager to spend time with baby Gigi, and the day came when your father refused to wait any longer. We agreed he would go ahead, and when Tomaso was six months old, I promised I would bring Tomaso and Nonna, and we would join him.

"In the moment that I made the promise, I wasn't sure I would keep it. But from the day he left our village, I missed your father terribly. By the time Tomaso was six months, I was excited about the journey. That much I remember.

"Of the ship, I remember almost nothing and no one. I am not even sure how it happened. Tomaso was strong and healthy, sitting up on our bunk and drooling because of his new teeth. He was such a happy baby; I think he understood we were going to find his Papa. But then one night, I woke up to feel him burning beside me, hot as an iron with fever. It was the first time he had ever been sick, and I didn't know what to do. I woke Nonna. She was very calm. We gave him water by the spoonful, but he would not drink and he would not nurse.

"There was a doctor on board the ship. He said to take the baby up outside, up into the air, and the cold sea air would help to cool his fever. I held him and walked the deck. I held on to ropes and rails with one arm when the ship rolled, and I would not go back inside. He was so thin and light in my arms; I thought the wind might carry him away. So I held him tighter—to keep him with me.

"As long as I could.

"Tomaso died in my bunk, three days before we arrived in America.

"I remember all that every day. And one thing more. The night he died, I heard the song of a concertina in the dark. Sweet, perfect music—as only an angel can make. And I listened to this song, again and again, as Tomaso's soul left me for paradise."

I was crying before she finished, and she held out her arms. She rocked me, like I'd seen her rock Emelina after a nightmare, and I buried my head in her pillow. I cried for her story, and I cried because I knew where her angel's song came from, but it seemed to me that to tell her would only open her wound wider, and I wanted it to heal. Mamma cried, too, the same as me—loud—as if it were something the neighbors, everyone, should hear.

"I think it will be easier now," said Mamma after a long time. She sighed. She sounded very tired, but her voice was steady and I knew she was my Mamma again—not a spirit lost on the moon. She was so real again that her stomach growled loudly. She smiled a little and patted it. "That, I am sure, was loud enough for your Papa to hear. Do you think you could make me some toast?"

I was still trembling from crying so much, and so was Mamma. I'm not sure where the joke in toast was, but all of a sudden she was laughing and so was I.

"But, Mamma! There's no bread!" And that was even funnier. We laughed at least as long as we cried, and then Mamma said never mind, she would rather have soup. But of course that was all gone, too. So she went through a whole list of ideas and discovered we had nothing but scraps of cold chicken and some stale crackers. And then I remembered the jar of Marmite from Dot. I told her it was smelly and salty and rotten and bad—she was right; it *was* crazy English food. And she said that sounded just perfect, and I should bring up the whole jar, and a spoon.

The next day, sometime after we had all gone to school, Mamma stepped back into our lives. When we got home she was in the kitchen, pouring batter onto the pizzelle iron. Emelina was sitting on the floor, an arm wrapped around one of Mamma's legs. In her free hand she had a fresh pizzelle. She was eating it the way she always did pizzelle—as if it were a flattened flower, which is what they look like, and only by carefully nibbling around the waffled edges, spiraling gradually into the center.

Most of Mamma was there. She was wearing

an apron over her navy blue town dress, and had red lipstick on, which she only wore when she went out. But I noticed right away what was missing. Her hair, her blonde coronet, was gone; what remained fit like a cap over her head. It was pretty, ringed by three tight waves about halfway down, the way other women in the neighborhood wore their hair.

"Mamma gotta wave!" Emeline announced to Sonia and me. And Mamma turned to look at us over her shoulder.

"Wha' you think? Is call-a marcel wave. You girls like it?"

"You look like a fashion model, Mamma!" shouted Sonia with excitement. "But where are your braids?"

"I sol' to da barber," said Mamma, and shrugged her shoulders lightly, as if it were only a trifling matter.

She patted her new hair, blushed, and looked pleased. Her face no longer bore the bluish tint of moonlight (although the lipstick made her skin look starkly white), and her cheeks were rosy from standing over the steaming hot iron. She looked relieved, like someone who had been carrying a pack that was too heavy and had finally taken it off.

"Wha-da you think your father gonna say?" she bit her lower lip, to hint she might be nervous, but she didn't seem seriously worried—her eyes were full of life. I could tell she was excited.

And then I realized the marvel she had just performed—everything she'd said since we came home was in English.

Papa's bootsteps landed on the back stairs and he opened the door. We all looked at him, to see his reaction. Papa's face broke into a look of relief and happiness. He swallowed and made a kind of whooping sound.

"He'll say, '*Magnifico!* (Magnificent!) What a beautiful wife I have!'"

Papa didn't stop to take off his boots and

coat. He took a couple of steps over, scooped Mamma up, and swung her around. She clung to him for a moment, then patted his back, as if he were a baby that needed calming down.

After dinner, while everyone was still in the living room, I told them I was going upstairs to practice. As I climbed the stairs, I decided to check something first. I slipped into my parents' room and pulled the suitcase out from under the bed. It felt lighter. And I knew without opening it that it was empty. And when I lifted the lid, I saw that I was right.

Mamma had finally unpacked.

CHAPTER 23

Flavia's Wedding

IMAGINE MY EMBARRASSMENT!
The Vancouver Sun, April 15, 1939

In January, my grandmother gave me my grandfather's accordion, even though I wanted a piano. You may not know this when you listen to the Coccola brothers play a concert on the radio, but the accordion is a very difficult instrument. With mine, there are 48 piano keys for the right hand to learn and 96 bass buttons for the left and you have to keep it breathing, moving in and out as you play, or it will only wheeze for you and not make music. It is also very heavy, as heavy as my three-year-old sister.

My mother is a seamstress and she makes the most beautiful wedding dresses, everyone says so.

One of her customers heard that I played the accordion and asked me to play at her wedding. My mother said yes, for me.

My whole family was invited to the wedding banquet. It was in the bride's parents' house. To make room, they took the doors between the dining room and the living room off their hinges and set up little tables. After dinner, everyone went downstairs to hear me play.

I only sort-of knew one song. I'd been practicing it for weeks, and on the day of the wedding I still hadn't really got it right. I was supposed to play "Drink to Me Only with Thine Eyes." My father carried my accordion down the stairs and lifted it up so I could put it on, while everyone leaned against the walls and each other and waited for something really nice to come out of the accordion.

But when I started to play, it was so terrible that I thought I would die on the spot. I tried to start again, and that might have been better, except that, my cousin, three-year-old Giulietta,

and my baby sister, Emelina, who nobody was pay-
ing attention to, came running into the room. They
were both STARK NAKED, and I do mean they
had not a stitch on. The whole room exploded in
laughter as my mother and my aunt chased the
girls around trying to catch them.

Can you just Imagine My Embarrassment?
Submitted by M. Benetti, age 11, Vancouver City

Of course, there was more to it than that.
Because I couldn't sleep after Flavia's wedding, I
had gone down to the kitchen and written a
three-page account of the whole awful event. I
thought it sounded very dull, the way the paper
changed it, and not like I'd written it at all.
Except that my name was at the bottom. So all I
could hope was that everyone at the wedding
read the Italian papers, not the *Sun*.

They cut out all the stuff about how Flavia
and Elmo were supposed to have a big banquet
in the Silver Slipper Hall, like the other rich

Italians did. But then there was some big secret fight in the family, so she ended up having people come to her house. And most of them weren't even her friends, but friends of her father's business, like Uncle Tony and our family. We were invited because Mamma had sewn all Flavia's best clothes since she had been a little girl, and had made her wedding dress.

And they took out the part about how Flavia's tummy made the front of her dress poke out, like there was someone caught in a curtain behind a stage. Or how Elmo spent most of the reception outside on the porch, smoking cigarettes with the old men and looking grouchy. And the good part, about how we ate antipasto and chicken and vegetables and pasta. And how there were all sorts of cookies and little cakes from the bakery for dessert. And how there was champagne for the grown-ups, and Sonia drank two juice glasses of red wine. And how, after dinner, she ran around collecting the pink streamer decorations and tying them into her hair. And how she told everyone she was a mermaid until she got tired and fell asleep under the buffet table, where nobody could find her. And how I felt sick from having snuck into the bathroom before dinner and eaten half a jar of Marmite for courage— which didn't make me brave (only thirsty). And how, when I came out, all the 7Up was gone, so I drank a glass of the wine, too, and then I felt like a *stupidobooby* right away, and all I wanted was to hide and take a nap like Sonia.

After I played—just thunking through the song and forgetting to squeeze after a couple of bars—I felt betrayed by everybody. Gioseff had promised me I'd see them clap and tap their feet in time. And when I saw the foot-tapping, that's how I'd know I had them with me, and I would know the joy of a real musician. Except everybody looked uncomfortable, like they'd sat in something sticky and were afraid to move. And nobody clapped because I didn't really make time they could follow. And nobody tapped their feet, except for Mrs. Antonelli. But she was just impatient—all rolling her eyes to God and looking like she wanted it to be over with. And then the streaking thing happened with Emelina and Giulietta, and everyone broke up, laughing and chasing them like they were chubby little piglets let loose in a barn.

The paper got it all wrong. It wasn't my little sister streaking that was my embarrassment—it was that, afterward, I couldn't stand how everybody avoided me. And people lied and said things like, "You'll get better," but their eyes all said, "Poor kid." So I went upstairs to hide under the buffet, which is when I lifted the tablecloth and found Sonia. Finally, Papa said we could go home. As we were putting on our coats, I could hear piano music from the Antonelli's parlor and murmurs of "So nice, so nice. Thassa beautiful song, Gigi. Play sommore."

I thought about all of this as I clipped out the

story before Sonia could see it. I thought I'd be smart about it, so I cut out the recipe and the travel diary someone had written that surrounded the column, and it wouldn't look like all I had taken was the "Imagine My Embarrassment" column. Because, for sure, Papa would ask about it, and like we said when Emelina went to the bathroom, *it was my private business.*

When I'd read the piece for the third time, I noticed the story beside it. It was the travel diary about some man's trip to Germany, and how he'd seen signs over the doors over many of the shops and hotels that said Jews Forbidden or Jews Not Welcome. But then he said how fond of music the Bavarians were, and how they would cheerfully serve you just a cup of coffee, even if that was all you ordered in a restaurant.

I made it to the mailbox first every day, until my dollar arrived from the newspaper a week later. I felt a little better. It amazed me how people would pay a whole dollar for a miserable little story of humiliation, but when Gioseff played his beautiful music in the train station, people only tossed him pennies. I wondered about that for a minute, maybe two, and then I went to look for the day's paper, to see if Woolworth's had roller skates on sale.

CHAPTER 24

A Coward in Disguise

THE FIRST CRACK SOUNDED like a hailstone against my accordion case. I knew I was in the danger zone—only a few steps from Mrs. Porchenski's front walk—and I knew it wasn't hail that hit. I looked back at the case. There was a tear where it had been struck; it looked like it had been slashed by a bear claw.

Thwack!

The second stone hit harder; and another gash, deeper than the first, scarred the center of my case. What had Nonna said? *Dis notta toy. Notta mark onnit. All perfetto, juss-a like new.*

Oh, Nonna. Not anymore.

I looked up at Dennis's window and my eyes narrowed. I should've kept moving, but I knew he was there. I knew it was him. What was it

Papa said about Mussolini? A bully is a coward in disguise. But if Mussolini were secretly a coward, and what the papers said was true; he sure was good at getting his own way.

Was I a coward without disguise? If only I'd had roller skates, I could've zipped by Mrs. Porchenski's before Dennis could take aim. I thought of Nonna, and how she'd taken such good care of my grandfather's one and only treasure. And I felt mad. How dare he? So I stood there in that little square of pavement, held my eyebrows together in a look of my father's, and stared down the whole of Mrs. Porchenski's house.

Go on, Dennis, I dare you. I double dare you. Throw one more rock and I'll…

I'll….

What would I do? Bash him with my accordion? In my mind, I heard the sound of angry, clashing chords as I swung it at him—the kind of sounds I made with it when I couldn't do anything else. And the sound and picture in my head were so awful they made me afraid of myself. I shivered and tried to shake off the thought. But I couldn't pretend I didn't have it. Was that murderous thinking, in the eyes of God? How could I even confess it?

Maybe he got bored with me just standing there, staring up at his window with my fierce face. I saw something coming at me, but there was no time—the rock hit me on the temple, beside my right eye. I doubled back, fell against the wagon, and crumbled over in a heap, the accordion crashing against me. I lay there for a second and felt like I'd been pasted to the side-walk. The wagon was knocked on its side when I fell over it, and the accordion landed hard in the gutter. Someone must have seen, but nobody came outside to help me.

"Ha! Bullseye! Gotcha good, s'getti head!" A shot of spit arced down from the roof and landed with a splat on the pavement where I'd stood only a moment before. I looked up dizzily and finally saw him. I'd been looking in the wrong place; he was on the roof, a slingshot in one hand, his mouth working up to gob again.

Whoever said that bunk about sticks and stones had never been hit in the head with a rock from Dennis Lister's slingshot. My head was throbbing, and I touched it—blood on my fingers.

"I kin see your underwear!" Dennis cawed and spat. It hit my shoe. I felt sick. My old instinct just to get out of Dennis's firing range came back in a rush. I rolled over and pushed myself up. For a second I thought I might faint. And then I realized how mad I still was. I took a deep breath and yanked the wagon upright, then, with one swinging motion, heaved the accordion case back onto it.

Only when I was at the foot of Mrs. Secco's stairs did I realize I'd never been able to lift the accordion that high before. I relied on Papa to put it in the wagon—and on Gioseff at the other end. My legs were shaking and I was crying even before I sat down on the bottom step.

"*Per amor di Dio!* (For the love of God!) Mariangela, what happened?"

Gioseff ran down the stairs, took one look at me, and called for Mrs. Secco. The next thing I knew, she was dabbing at my skinned knees while Gioseff was holding a folded rag to the cut on my head.

With all my baby sobs you'd think it would've come out right then. All Dennis's small tortures, and then this one, which would surely leave a scar everyone could see. How could I explain the gash in my head without telling the truth? I could make believe Gioseff was my big brother, my hero; he would deal with Dennis.

But all I could say was, "I fell down." And when Gioseff asked again, squeezing my shoulders, insisting, imploring—all I would say was, "I fell down. The accordion knocked me over."

Finally, he gave up asking.

I was too shaky for a lesson. And Gioseff seemed unsure of what to do with me. Mrs. Secco gave me a clean padded cloth to hold against my head, and Gioseff took the Camroni out of its case.

He held it, stroked it a little, and talked to it, looking it over as if it too had been injured and was only hiding the wound from view. "Let's see how you sound," said Gioseff to the accordion as he gently slipped on the straps. He fiddled with scraps of different tunes, and tested each key and button, before he was at last satisfied the Camroni was unharmed.

"It would take more than a fall off a wagon to knock the music out of you," he said approvingly to the accordion, but he raised an eyebrow at me.

And then we sat in Mrs. Secco's parlor, and Gioseff just played—songs I'd never heard from him before. Songs I didn't know from anywhere. He danced and stomped. He whirled the room into a frenzy. And when I closed my eyes I saw a room full of instruments, and Gioseff was playing them all. And whether or not they were meant to, every song raged with anger—the kind of music you'd play before you went to war.

CHAPTER 25

Sticks and Stones and Wagon Bones

LATER, GIOSEFF ASKED IF HE COULD walk me home. I lied. I told him I wasn't going home; I was having supper at Dot's house, and she only lived around the corner.

I don't know why I lied. What surprised me more was that Gioseff seemed to believe me.

"Okay, then. See you next week. Save the dollar for another time."

I trudged off, and wondered if Gioseff noticed that I crossed the street to walk on the other side.

As soon as Dennis's house came into sight, I scanned the roof, window, and front porch. There was no sign of him. Maybe he was having dinner. I thought my chances were good, even though I couldn't see the other gable. I looked around. The street was empty—if I ran the block in time, maybe I could make it home without him spotting...

Thwack!

My ankle! The pain was incredible; it felt like I'd been struck by an arrow, right to the bone. I let go of the wagon, hugged my knee to my chest, and hopped on my good leg, trying to make my body forget.

All of a sudden I heard a rush come up from behind me. Someone grabbed me. I screamed.

"Mariangela! You okay?" It was Gioseff. "Can you stand on it?"

Gingerly I lowered my foot. My ankle throbbed, but it didn't hurt to stand on.

"I saw the whole thing. Wait here!" Gioseff tore across the street and up Mrs. Porchenski's steps to her front door. Then he swung open the door and ran inside, as if he lived there and was desperate for the toilet. I saw him disappear inside and, just as quickly, he was back again— with Dennis Lister thrashing about in his arms.

"Getcher stinkin' hands off me, ya crazy three-fingered Wop!" screamed Dennis, flailing his arms like a chicken in a trap. Gioseff was breathing hard, but he didn't seem to have any trouble holding Dennis. It was like watching a movie. I was so fascinated with what might come next that I forgot to be afraid. My head cleared and I stood up straight.

Gioseff held Dennis in a headlock as he yanked him across the street. He brought him right up to me and then stopped. Close enough to spit.

"You had enough of this, Mariangela? You wanna punch him? You go ahead; I'll hold him." Gioseff's mouth was wrenched taut into a grimace. I could see his teeth as he panted and hung on, while Dennis struggled against him. Gioseff yanked him up so hard that Dennis's shirt got hiked up over his skinny ribs and belly button.

And I wondered—looking at him, seeing how puny he was—how I'd ever been afraid of him.

I nodded my head. Dennis's eyes widened. I felt my hands ball into fists. And then we were surrounded by this sharp, sour smell. Pee. Dennis's pants were wet and clinging to his legs. His nose was running and he was crying. It was like I had actually hit him. I held my fists up to his face, right close to his eyes. I didn't know what I was going to do next. But when I saw his slingshot dangling from out of his back pocket, I dropped my fists and grabbed it. It was surprisingly flimsy, just a little piece of badly whittled wood, not much bigger than a turkey wishbone.

I tossed it on the ground, picked up the handle of my wagon and pulled the wheels over the slingshot. When that didn't break it, I wrapped my arms around my accordion case, lifted it up, and brought it down, hard, on Dennis' prized weapon.

Pulverized! And with only one smash! A wave of gratitude for the accordion came over me. What had Gioseff's friend said? When you need her, she will come to your rescue.

I looked back at Gioseff. Dennis had stopped struggling and now was just bawling.

"What's her name?" Gioseff barked, shaking Dennis.

"Huh?"

"What's…her…name!" Gioseff lifted up Dennis's dribbly chin, to face me. He looked like he had no idea what Gioseff was saying.

"No more Spaghetti Benetti. No more Dago. No more Wop." With every name he reeled off, Gioseff gave Dennis another shake.

"Her name is Mariangela. Say it!"

Dennis mumbled something that sounded like *Mbbleanjellah*.

"Louder!" Another shake.

"Mariangela!"

Gioseff let go. Dennis stumbled but caught himself before he fell into the little pool that had collected round his feet. He looked drained, which he kind of was, since his pants were sticky with pee. I thought he'd run away, but he just stood there.

"From now on, that's the only name you call her. *Capisci?* (Understand?)"

Dennis nodded, and Gioseff gave him a little shove to get him moving.

"And, Dennis?" growled Gioseff.

Dennis stopped in the middle of the street. With his back to us, he stood there, his shoulders down, defeated—but listening.

"Say it nice."

We stood there and watched. Dennis walked slowly to his house, up the stairs, and closed the door behind him.

I turned to Gioseff, afraid to see his angry face again. But all I saw was my gentle teacher. He pulled a folded handkerchief from his pocket and mopped his brow. He saw me looking at him and smiled gently.

"I've known about him for a while. I followed you home the first few lessons, just to make sure you made it okay. Sorry. I didn't want to interfere." He lifted my accordion onto the wagon.

Gioseff reached out and gave me an awkward pat on the shoulder. "It's over now. You don't have to worry about him anymore."

It wasn't over, though. I still had Mamma to tell.

CHAPTER 26

Open the Windows

MAMMA LEANED ACROSS the dinner table. She smoothed my hair back from the side of my face to expose the swollen cut. She held her hand there and spoke sharply to Papa.

"Look, Orazio! Look what that Lister boy did to Mariangela!"

Papa got up and came to inspect the gash.

"She could'a lost an eye!" Mamma cried shrilly. *"Che imbecille!"*

Papa held my chin between his thick, calloused fingers and looked me sternly in the eyes. "Mariangela? You do something to this boy? You call him names? Make fun of him?"

"No, Papa. Nothing. Nothing at all."

I felt angry. How could he even ask me that? All of a sudden, my parents' united front was split down the center, like the wide crack in the wood of our table. "Orazio, why she gotta learn *fisarmonica*?"

"What's this got to do with accordion?" asked Papa.

Mamma gave me a you-explain-it-just-like-you-told-me look. Papa let go of my face, sat back down, pushed his plate forward roughly, and clasped his hands in front of him on the table. He waited.

"I go by his house to lessons. He spits sometimes. Calls me names."

"What kind of names?"

I tried to think of the mildest ones, the ones that bothered me the least.

"Spaghetti Benetti. Eye-talian. Dumb stuff, Papa. It's not so bad."

Sonia decided I wasn't making the point well enough on my own.

"He calls her Frog Eye-talian! Gypsy! Bug-eyes! Circus freak!"

"Circus freak?"

How Sonia knew all this, I had no idea.

"Because of the accordion—he thinks Mariangela should run away and join the circus."

Papa looked pained.

Mamma took a sharp breath. "It's enough already, Orazio. She could-a lost an eye. An eye! Is crazy—this accordion. She play terrible. Is no worth it."

It was an out, an escape route from the accordion lessons and the awful practices. No more performing at weddings. I could trade back my promise to Father Paul for Hail Marys.

I should have felt relieved—at last the key to my freedom was dangling within my reach. But then I realized that it was not because of Dennis that Mamma wanted me to stop. It was because I really *was* bad. I mean, I always knew I was bad, but Mamma saying it made it true.

"She can learn. You gotta be patient, Carmella! Music is the way to a better life. All this money for lessons—just so she can quit? That's no good."

"You girls clear the table." Papa got up and headed for the landing. Mamma was right behind him. They stomped upstairs to argue in their bedroom. Loud. All in Italian. Downstairs, we ran around to check that all the windows were closed.

It was Mamma who came to tell me. Long after I should have been asleep, she opened the bedroom door and whispered, in the way a sister would, "Mariangela, you 'wake?"

I hesitated.

"Yes, Mamma."

I looked at her, with her sleek new hairstyle, silhouetted in the hall light. I missed her long blonde hair—brushed out from its braids and flowing, when she came to tuck us in at night. Her beauty seemed more ordinary now. And I realized that I had been proud she was different from other mothers. I felt sorry she looked more like them now.

I knew what she was going to say, even before she spoke. I'd heard the whole argument. While I eavesdropped, I thought of how the newspaper reported that thirteen-year-old Princess Elizabeth was already being trained to be queen. It was not so terrible to be queen, except that nobody asked the first-born if she wanted to be queen. Just like they don't ask if you want to learn your grandfather's accordion. They just thump you with it when you reach, like the paper called it, *the awkward age*—to make sure you really and truly *have* an awkward age.

Then I thought of my Nonna, and how disappointed she'd be—how she'd have to pin her hopes on Sonia—or wait a long time for Emelina to grow big enough. I thought of Gioseff, and the dollar a week. What if he were saving up so he could marry Sabina? But mostly I thought of how he played. And I wondered— what if I held on just long enough, to find out if I had just a little of what he had? Could I make people feel the way he did? And I thought about Dennis, and how great it would be, never to walk past his house again. But I'd still have to see him in school, so what would I really gain?

"Your father says no more accordion lessons. You can tell Gioseff tomorrow."

I'd waited a long time for my salvation. Too long—because now Mamma was too late. As soon as she offered me my freedom, I knew I wasn't going to quit. I would learn a whole song, melody and bass, and then I'd make up my mind about it.

"Mamma? If it's okay with you, I think I'll keep at it a while longer. I can practice in the cowshed if you want." In the dark, I sounded very certain—in the same way that Emelina told us she had counted a million ladybugs one night, in a dream.

Mamma had to muffle a laugh, and Papa stuck his head in the doorway. I didn't know he'd been standing there.

"Mariangela, you play like your Mamma speaks English. Maybe terrible, but it sounds good to me. Practice anywhere you want. Living room, kitchen, bathroom, cowshed...wherever you like...open the window, we're proud of you...let the neighbors hear!"

They both came in and kissed me on the forehead, like they used to when I was very small. Mamma touched the cut on my temple in her magic way. She made me believe my lump would not scar—it would be gone by morning. I thought of how she and Gioseff shared part of the same story, and I wondered if I should tell her after all. It seemed like the right time. But if she had wanted to recognize him, it would have happened the day he first auditioned for my parents. When Mamma and Papa slipped out of the room together, I was glad I hadn't said anything after all. Then I closed my eyes and imagined I was flying on roller skates to my lesson.

And I fell asleep smiling in the dark.

CHAPTER 27

Semplice

GETTING TO MY LESSON was a breeze on my new roller skates. I pulled my wagon right past Mrs. Porchenski's house without even a flinch at the thought of Dennis. No more dragging the wagon—we glided along like water on glass. No more stopping to pull up my stockings. If it wasn't for the curbs, I could've rolled all the way there, like a ribbon unraveling in the wind.

For my first lesson in April, Gioseff wasn't in his parlor or his room when I got there. I found him on Mrs. Secco's back deck. He was outlining letters on an enormous banner.

"What's it for?" I panted, breathless from lugging the accordion up the stairs by myself.

"The king and queen," said Gioseff, standing back and tucking his pencil behind his ear.

He took out a piece of paper and showed me the words he'd begun to copy:

TO THEIR MOST GRACIOUS MAJESTIES
ON THIS HISTORIC OCCASION,
THE ITALIAN COLONY OFFER
A SINCERE TRIBUTE OF LOYALTY & DEVOTION

Gloryosky. That was grand.

I felt proud of him, doing this for the king and queen. Something of Gioseff would be part of history, even if no one knew it. Too bad they wouldn't hear him play the accordion—too bad for them.

"That's a lot of words to paint," I said stupidly.

"Yes. Yes, it is."

Gioseff pulled up a stool and sat down in front of me. His brow was creased from concentrating on the banner, I thought, and he looked serious.

Gioseff took a deep breath and clasped his hands together. "Mariangela, I've gotta apologize to you."

"What for?"

"It's just that I don't think I can teach you the accordion."

I couldn't believe it. Not teach me? What did he mean, not teach me?

"Why not?" I barely choked out.

"Well, we've tried it for four months now, and it's just..." Gioseff struggled for the words.

"I'm terrible?"

Gioseff nodded. *"Terribile."*

Well, that was nothing new. Everybody thought I was *terribile*. And now, even my teacher admitted it. But with teachers, there had to be some rule—they couldn't just dump you. Could they?

"A dollar's a lot of money," Gioseff said. "You could get lessons downtown at Paramount Studios for that, from a professional teacher."

I was unteachable. A musical dunce. How was I going to explain this to my parents? I sat there for a second in silence. I couldn't believe

I'd dragged that stupid case up all those stairs, just to have Gioseff cut me loose. Dumped. It sounded like something out of a bizarre Dorothy Dix column.

"But…" I wanted to argue. I was going to argue. I wanted to ask for one more try. Another couple of weeks. A different song… I was thinking so hard, to come up with something, that I closed my eyes—which is when I saw an old man's face, calm and patient, appear in my mind. I recognized him without ever having known him. Nonno.

"Gioseff…"

"Yes?"

"Your father never read music, did he?"

"No. No he didn't."

"Neither did my grandfather."

Gioseff looked surprised.

"If he didn't read music, how did he teach you?"

Gioseff blinked. He looked away from me, across the porch and out, over the lane and away into the distance. Like Mamma, when she went back. One side of his mouth curled up in a half smile.

"No books, no reading, just note by note. One note at a time. Over and over and over again. He played; I copied him until we had a song. *Semplice* (Simple)."

The guilty look on Gioseff's face vanished and his eyes sparkled. He knocked the base of his palm against his forehead and laughed.

"Lemme get my accordion. I'll be right back." He leapt up and disappeared through the kitchen. I could hear him hustle upstairs as I snapped the locks on my case open, lifted the lid, and whisked the velvet cloth over the Camroni's ivory keys.

"Thank you, Nonno," I whispered. "Thank you very much."

That afternoon, Gioseff gave me six notes and two base chords—the beginning of a folk song from his village. I copied him until my wrists ached and my neck was sore from the weight of the accordion. That was it, the whole lesson.

"Come back tomorrow, and Friday, too." Gioseff ordered. "No charge. Just come." And in the coming weeks, he squeezed in extra lessons and I squeezed out new notes.

I practiced every day with determination. And every time I launched in, I thought about my Nonna, while she cooked risotto, reminding God, "You gotta keep stirring or it'll stick to the pot."

I worked hard to keep my fingers moving. I stopped counting every finger slip, every missed note. I stirred the song, one snippet at a time. Gioseff doled out a little more each week. And I strung it together, the way Mamma filled a line with laundry.

A month went by. I learned the whole village song, then "Dreaming," "You Are My Heart," and "Beautiful Brown Eyes"—all the same way.

Sometimes, at the beginning of a new song, I thought I'd go crazy—six notes one day, twelve more the next, then twenty-four the week after, until I had a melody. But note by note, I kept stirring; and if I got stuck, I dug in and kept moving.

The music was a mountain. Keep moving. Don't fall off.

Four songs in four weeks.

A repertoire.

In my house, everyone heard me practice. The upstairs bedrooms were too warm to keep the windows shut all afternoon, so the neighbors heard me, too. But I gave my first official concert to Emelina, Billydog, and Hippo-the-Potamus.

"How did it sound?" I asked her, a little nervously after I'd played "Beautiful Brown Eyes."

What if I was wrong? What if I didn't have it?

Emelina did not answer at first. She sat and stared at the floor. I could see her brow furrow, and her face took on an expression that everyone in my family had in common, at one time or another—the look of serious searching for the perfect word.

Then, with great certainty, she latched upon it.

"Magnifico!" She nodded her head. And then she clapped crazily, missing her hands a couple of times. She smiled up at me, loving the word she offered. "Oh, *magnifico!"*

Emelina-*inglesina*...who never spoke Italian.

CHAPTER 28

Two-oh-seven . . .

ALMOST EVERY DAY, stories in the newspaper crept closer and closer to announcing the king and queen's arrival in Canada. We read about the man who was chosen to be the king's barber on the tour and about children, practicing their curtseys and how to address the king (Sir) and queen (your Majesty), if they were introduced. I read aloud to Mamma that the queen's fashions were to be mostly blue crepe de Chine (some in lilac and lavender), with gray and white fox furs for trimming.

I read every story, usually twice. I was fascinated by George and Elizabeth—what power they had to be able to push Hitler and Mussolini off the front pages! I loved them for it. Papa said perhaps things were not so terrible in Europe after all.

But after reading the story about the children

who had been chosen to give bouquets to the queen at City Hall, Sonia lost all interest in the tour. She stopped pasting the stories into her scrapbook. Instead she fussed over the comics and who was going to adopt the orphan, Little Annie Rooney. Would it be kind old Mr. Barnes? Mr. and Mrs. Warde, who were very rich? The hard-working Mrs. McMack?—as long as it wasn't the sneaky Mrs. Flowers. Annie Rooney used to be my favorite, too. But she really was a little twit if she couldn't see that Mrs. Flowers was pure wickedness.

Sonia stuck her Annie Rooney comics in her new book alongside funny advertisements, like the one for Lifebuoy Soap, where the man was just about to propose to his girlfriend but "B.O. came between them."

I clipped the serial biography of the queen; the pictures of the princesses and their parents greeting the crowds, who had come to see them off on May the 6th; and the sketches of copies of the queen's dresses and furs, which were for sale downtown. There was even a report that the king and queen would see two movies on their way to Canada—*Jesse James* and a Charlie Chan picture. I clipped that, too, and wondered if they had any say in what they saw. Somehow the choices didn't seem very royal.

I didn't have a scrapbook of my own, so I just stuffed the clippings in my accordion case. I figured Sonia would get over her snit and want them someday.

Even Emelina was busy with the newspaper. As Papa had learned his English, Emelina was learning her numbers. Sonia had trained her to read out loud the winning number of the Lucky Badge Contest every day. Then Sonia would tell us what movie tickets the winners would receive: *Gunga Din; The Little Princess,* with Shirley Temple; Mickey Rooney in *The Adventures of Huckleberry Finn.* I barely listened—I'd pretty much forgotten I even had a Lucky Badge number.

The day the ocean liner *Empress of Australia* sailed for Canada with the king and queen aboard, Mamma was so busy sewing for the neighborhood that Nonna had to come and cook for us again. Mamma had accepted an order from Mr. Zucchi for fifty Union Jack beanies—for boys. "The old *Pidocchioso*! I charge him double!" we heard her tell Papa. After that, Mamma sewed traditional Italian girls' costumes—white peasant blouses with puffed sleeves, black lace-up waist-coats, and flouncy skirts patterned with flowers or stripes. She said she'd make us matching out-fits, but the orders kept coming in from other mothers, so there wasn't time.

"The baker's children are starving," joked Papa in a sing-song voice, the way he always did when Mamma was at her busiest. "The shoe-maker's children have no shoes."

This suited Emelina very well. She declared she was going "nekkid" and started to pull her dress over her head.

"I don't think so," said Mamma in her that's-the-end-of-that voice. Mamma frowned fiercely at Emelina until she pulled her dress back down. Then she stomped on the pedal of her sewing machine and told us we all had plenty of clothes, and we could wear our new Easter hats the day the king and queen came to Vancouver.

Mamma sighed over Queen Elizabeth's costumes. I found her own sketches of them on the pad of paper she kept near the telephone. But she acted like all the fuss about wearing Italian costumes was silly. "Who's gonna see three little girls in the crowd, Orazio?" she countered my father.

Nonna agreed with Mamma, and added her own two cents. "There are some distances that can't be crossed."

My father said how we presented ourselves sent a message—we had to show the king and queen that Italy was not all fascist Mussolinis. We could be Italian and call the Dominion our home. We could be proud to have a king and queen, but also be proud of our roots.

"Where you are born is like your mother," said Papa. "You grow up, maybe you leave her for a new home, but she's always in your heart."

Nonna, who was washing the dishes, said, wryly, that he could tell that to Tony and Letizia, since they still lived with her. Mamma and Papa thought that was very funny.

"Maybe now it's time for my surprise," said Papa, getting up from his chair. Everyone looked up.

"Surprise! Yay!" shouted Emelina, and scrambled up to Papa. He carried her into the kitchen and down the stairs to the basement. When they came back, Emelina was wearing a Union Jack beanie on her head and waving three Union Jack flags. Papa was holding a plain brown paper bag. Sonia grabbed for it, but Papa held it just above her reach.

"Maybe your mother's right," he said. "Maybe our king and queen will not see the

Benetti girls. But with these, from wherever you are, you'll surely see them!"

He then let Emelina rip open the bag. Inside were three identical cardboard Dominion Periscopes. Emelina and Sonia played submarine until bedtime.

Every day, as the royal ocean liner steamed closer to Canada, the waiting got harder to bear. I felt antsy in school. I was so restless and fidgety that I practiced endless accordion fingerings on my desk. Then came the news that the *Empress* had been slowed down by fog, and for a couple of days, I wondered if they would ever make it to Canada at all.

At night, instead of practicing my accordion, I helped Mamma sew. But now I felt impatient to get practicing again. I worried that my repertoire would slip and I'd lose my little bit of music, so hard won. I did fingerings on the kitchen table at suppertime until Mamma poked my hand with a fork and told me to sit still before I drove her crazy. So I just practiced on my legs under the tablecloth instead. And late at night, when Emelina and Sonia were asleep, I crawled out our window to practice on the roof of the cowshed.

On May the 16th, the day before the *Empress of Australia* was to arrive in Quebec, I cut out a story about the king and queen's first meals in Canada—for lunch, iced melon, squab chicken, new beans, shoestring potatoes, and *soufflé glaçée au Grand Marnier*; and for dinner, caviar, consommé, trout, spring lamb, champagne sherbet, and breast of snow birds. I told Sonia she should try drawing all that for Miss Snively, and tell her it was what we eat every Sunday. That would impress the boots off her, for sure.

Sonia went straight for the comics page, where she and Emelina performed their nightly ritual, with bowed heads, over the Lucky Badge bulletin.

"Two…oh…seven…"

"That's right, now the rest," said Sonia, who loved playing teacher.

"Three…oh…three…"

"Two tickets for Merle Oberon and Laurence Olivier in *Wuthering Heights*," said Sonia, to no one in particular. "Huh! I'm glad I didn't win," she carried on. "I want tickets for Shirley Temple in *The Little Princess*. Not a weepy, kissy-face movie, with a lot of cryin' and carryin' on."

I thought Merle Oberon was beautiful. If Mamma would only let me pluck my eyebrows, I would do mine like Merle Oberon's—perfect arcs, each as thin as a pencil line. But I was sure Mamma hid the tweezers; I could never find them in the bathroom.

Dot swore she was in love with Laurence Olivier, even though he was always terribly serious-looking. Shirley Temple was for kids. I was almost halfway to twelve.

It took a moment for it to sink in.

207303.

My number.

And I wasn't even feeling lucky that day.

CHAPTER 29

Wednesday, May 17, 1939

THAT NIGHT I DREAMT in accordion.

I saw a baby with a tiny blue concertina that twinkled with paste-jewels. He played a little lullaby that my mother used to sing. Then there was Gioseff, playing a simple waltz outside Mr. Stefani's store. The streetlights flickered. The sky darkened and it was my grandfather, standing in a spotlight, in a work shirt, apron, and dark trousers held up by suspenders. Tiny round spectacles balanced on his forehead, and his eyes were wrinkled in joy. He played "Lady of Spain" on a bright red accordion with black buttons and creamy white keys. Nonna stood a little in front of him, singing. And finally I knew their secret: he played and she sang. And that was how they were perfect together.

Nonna's face faded away with the last notes of my grandfather's song. And so did he, but in a different way. He became younger. The wrinkles of his face smoothed clear, except around his eyes. And he was tall and straight and handsome, with his hair parted to one side, and a long, isosceles, English nose—the face from the one-cent postage stamp. He wore a tweed suit, white shirt, and dark tie. And he picked up the tune, where my grandfather had left off. Only now he was playing the "Sharpshooters March." The streetlights were gone. In an all-but-empty auditorium were the three of us—their Majesties King George and Queen Elizabeth, and myself.

On the edge of the stage, overlooking the orchestra pit, the queen and I perched on twin high-backed chairs. We wore silvery ball gowns. I had a tiara in my hair; she wore the circlet from her crown. She also wore an enormous diamond brooch. "The Koh-i-noor" she said, leaning toward me conspiratorially, and brushing the diamond lightly with one gloved finger.

"Mariangela," she said warmly, "I have heard..." She paused to think what it was, and I waited, unable to imagine what great news of me had traveled so far.

"I have heard," she began again, a smile showing her small teeth, "so very much about you."

My reputation had traveled all the way to Buckingham Palace? Me? How curious. How wonderful. How strange. And the queen spoke to me in Royal, which was very like English, I thought, only more posh.

She held out the back of one white-gloved hand. I hesitated and held tightly onto the edges of my chair. Was I supposed to shake her hand?

"The fingers," she whispered, making a tiny wave at the floor. "Just the fingers."

So I reached out, and we shook fingers very daintily, the queen and I.

There were little wheels on the bottoms of the chair legs and, using our feet, we twirled to the music coming up from the orchestra pit. The king was playing "Ciribiribin."

"Isn't he magnificent?" said the queen with gracious pride. "He plays so well, but no one ever hears." She was not speaking perfect Royal any longer. Instead, she became very chatty, speaking in plainer English—as if she'd just had an espresso.

"He is quite shy about everything, you know," she confided to me. "And in the palace, the sound would carry so frightfully far," she added. "It is hard to keep the accordion a secret. One can't be quiet about it, so one simply doesn't play."

I looked over at her and saw she was holding the little baby with the blue concertina on her knee. The baby joined the king in the song. His chubby little arms squeezed the bellows as naturally and happily as he might clap his hands. The queen seemed to like this very much, and she jounced the baby lightly to the time of the music.

My mother, pushing a pram, crossed the stage toward us. "Tomaso! There you are. Time for your nap," and she lifted him gently from the queen's lap and set him in the pram. The baby kept playing as my mother wheeled him away from us, and they disappeared into the wings. They took the last notes of "Ciribiribin" away with them. And the king was once again playing by himself, this time a song I didn't recognize.

"Ah! A Camroni! What a bright tone! There's no mistaking it for another, is there, Mariangela?"

"Mariangela?"

"Mariangela?"

"Listen, Mariangela," squealed Sonia, shaking my shoulders. "The bells! It means they're here! They've arrived!"

It was 7:30 in the morning, Wednesday, May 17. I had never heard such a glorious sound in the middle of the week before. All the bells, of all the churches, were ringing in the morning air. I thought hard for the words—*suono gioioso* (a joyous sound). The bells of Sacred Heart, and all the other East End churches, were ringing together so that everyone in the neighborhood would know the king and queen had stepped onto Canadian soil.

The royal tour had begun.

CHAPTER 30

Cleaning Up

"YOU'RE NOT GOING? What do you mean you're not going?"

Dot and Esther and I were sitting on the roof of the cowshed. I was wearing my accordion, and silently fingering "Will Ye No Come Back Again." I'd read that wherever the king and queen went, someone in the crowd would play this song as they were leaving, and everyone would sing. Bagpipers, fiddlers, tin whistlers, brass bands—all led the chorale at one time or another. But not once did the papers report an accordion in their midst. It got me thinking. The week before, I'd begged Gioseff to help me figure it out. I sang the melody as best I could, and from that Gioseff worked out the notes for the keys and taught it back to me. I stayed so long past the hour that Mrs. Secco finally stomped up the stairs and said, heavens to Betsy, that was surely enough for one day.

It was Sunday afternoon. The king and queen were to arrive the next morning. We were supposed to be making a plan to meet up, to watch the visit. Now Esther was backing out.

"I'm not going!" she said brightly, without a trace of regret in her voice. How could she not be disappointed?

"My cousins are in England. They made it out of Germany! We got a telegram from England yesterday. They're coming to live with us, so Mum and Dad say we have to clean up."

Esther was beaming. While Dot dreamed of falling in love, and I was more and more determined every day to win over my accordion, Esther's whole life's ambition was to clean up and have us over for lunch. Ironically, the one day of the year when laundry was banned from all clotheslines in the city (for fear it would detract from all the banners and bunting), Esther and her family were going to clean up. All I could think was, dreams really do come true. But that was too corny to say.

"I can't meet you, either," said Dot. "My dad is paying ten dollars a piece for us to have seats on the curb in front of the Hotel Vancouver, to see them when they go in to lunch."

It was hot on the cowshed, and I felt sweaty under the weight of the accordion. We had our skirts hitched up past our knees and were sipping cold apple juice we'd snuck out in mason jars. Down at the end of the alley, I saw someone walking toward us. His shoulders were hunched over and he had his hands stuffed in his pockets. He was still a few houses away when he stopped, saw me, and turned around.

Dennis.

He hadn't been in school for over a week.

He walked slowly to the corner of the alley, turned round the bend, and disappeared.

"Did'ja see? That was Dennis Lister," said Esther, pointing down the alley. "Did you hear about his mother?"

"No."

"She came back. She had TB and was in a sanitarium out in the valley."

"How do you know?" I asked, keeping watch on the alley in case Dennis reappeared. I wasn't afraid of him anymore, but he still made me a little nervous.

"My parents pick up more than junk," Esther shrugged. "They see stuff. My dad gave Mr. and Mrs. Lister and Dennis a ride home from the streetcar on the weekend. He couldn't have done it, except that they're all really skinny, especially her, so they squeezed in all right. He said they seemed like a really nice family. Dad said Dennis held on to his mother and cried the whole way home."

"He cries a lot," I blurted, and just behind the words I remembered the pact with Gioseff and Dennis. That clammed me up, sharp.

Dot was curious. "I've never seen him cry at school. He's the one who makes the other kids bawl. How do you know?"

I guess I could've betrayed him. Tell them how he peed his pants on the street and how I smushed his slingshot with my accordion. For sure he deserved it.

"I just do, that's all."

"Huh," said Dot, accepting there was nothing more to it than that. "Can you play us something now?"

"What do you want to hear?"

"'God Save the King.' You know it yet?"

I did.

CHAPTER 31

A Very Great Distance to Cross

HERE'S WHAT I WANT to remember forever.

How, the night before the train rolled into Vancouver, Emelina rolled out of bed and woke me up. Sonia never stirred. When I picked Emelina up and tucked her back in, I was surprised at how light she felt. My arms and back were strong from all the practicing.

I went back to bed, but I couldn't get back to sleep. Rain beat against the window and, in my head, the thought repeated itself tirelessly—what Nonna said about some distances that can't be crossed. How could she say that, when she'd traveled half the world to get here?

Finally I got up and went to the window. In

the pre-dawn light, I could just make out the shadows of people slowly making their way to the train station.

And I made up my mind.

I got dressed in the dark, put my accordion in its case, and snuck into the hall. It was hard to tiptoe down the stairs. A couple of times, the case slammed against my ankle bones, and I had to bite my lip to keep from crying out loud.

In the kitchen I scribbled a note on an old envelope:

Gone to see K & Q.
XOXO
M.

At the back door, the rain made me hesitate. I darted to the shed, got the accordion onto the wagon, and waited there a long time. Finally the downpour subsided to a sickly drizzle, and I could start down the lane. The accordion jostled behind me, jumpy in the wagon—jumpy like me.

I was about to turn the corner when I heard a voice behind me.

"Mariangela? Is that you?"

At first I didn't recognize him in the half light. He sounded hesitant, not at all like my tormentor of so many months. He took a few steps closer and peered at me.

"Yes."

Who else towed an accordion, by wagon, in our neighborhood?

Dennis Lister stepped awkwardly forward.

"D'ya need any help with that thing?"

"No. I'm good...thanks."

"'Kay." Dennis shoved his empty hands in his pockets, shuffled past me, and joined the dark, quiet stream of people. Just before he slipped out of sight I called out to him.

"Hey, Dennis! You want to borrow my periscope?"

I saw his back straighten. He turned and hurried back to me.

"You sure you don't want it?"

I shook my head and held it out. "I'm not gonna need it. Not where I'll be."

"Gee, thanks." Dennis reached out and grabbed the periscope—fast. Maybe he thought I'd change my mind. "I'll give it back to you at school tomorrow. Okay?"

Dennis hurried off down the dark alley.

The alley was uneven, and the accordion tipped and swayed, threatening to pitch itself into a puddle with every bump. It took me an eternity to make it to the paved sidewalk, where a thin, straggling row of dampened people filed by. Some were carrying camp stools; others had piano benches or lawn chairs. A few toted their seats in wagons, so nobody looked at me cross-eyed. I just joined in and we sleepily filed along to the railway station. People talked softly to one another or not at all. Little children, clutching miniature Union Jack flags, dozed on fathers' shoulders; mothers followed with picnic hampers.

As I walked, more of a plan came into my head. The royal train was still hours away; I would have a place to stand right in front, anywhere I wanted. But what I wanted was to get up high, above it all. And when I saw the fire escape of the Hotel Ivanhoe, I knew for sure where I was going. I just wasn't sure if I could get up there or not.

I tucked the wagon against the back wall of the hotel and lifted off the accordion case. I counted each step I took on the fire escape, and managed ten before I realized it was impossible. I'd have to lighten my load. So I opened the case and, as I did so, a little breeze came and caught all the clippings I'd saved for Sonia. They fluttered around my head in the early morning light, like feathers from a seagull in mid-flight, before a gust of wind swept them across the park toward the great station. I carefully slipped the accordion on my back, as if it were my school satchel, left the case where it was, and started to climb again.

I let myself rest every ten steps. By the time I reached the roof, my mouth was dry and I was gasping for air.

"You need some help with that, little lady?" said a big man, walking over from where a small group of people were clustered together, sitting on lawn chairs. They had lap rugs covering their legs, and some of them were smoking and chatting quietly. It was as if they just waiting for the party to begin, so they could start getting squiffy.

I let the man lift the accordion off my back. He was about to set it down on the roof, but there was so much grit and bird poop littering the ground that I panicked.

"No, wait!" And I whipped off my sweater and spread it out for the accordion. Only then did I realize how much my arms and back were hurting.

Now I didn't know what to do with myself. And I realized how alone I was. Everyone else seemed to be with somebody. And there I was, on my own. I was so exhausted, I despaired of why I'd even come. I sat down heavily on the case and waited for the feeling to return to my arms and legs.

"Give us a song, lovey," called a woman from behind me. "A song fit for a king!"

I couldn't move right away. My arms were nearly numb and my heart was still pounding in my ears from the climb. Maybe she thought I didn't hear her. Finally, with a faint prayer to Saint Cecilia, I lifted the accordion onto my lap. I ran my fingers up and down over a few scales and launched straight into "The Maple Leaf Forever." I didn't look at anyone. I couldn't. So I fixed my gaze across the buildings and to the mountains.

Can you hear me, Nonno? Am I high enough?

It felt magical, up there, as the sun rose around us. The clouds broke apart and the day grew brighter with what everyone had come to call the "king's weather."

When I finished, the gray-haired woman who had called for a song unwrapped a boiled egg and offered it to me, with a smile that showed one black gap in her front teeth. I realized I hadn't had any breakfast. The egg was delicious. I wolfed it down. The woman chuckled contentedly and held out the lid of her Thermos, filled with hot tea.

"Thank you," I said, and wrapped my hands around the cup.

"What's your name, dear?"

"Mariangela. Mariangela Benetti."

"'Ow long 'ave you played that?" she asked, nodding at the accordion.

"About five months."

"Well! Bless me! You're as fine a musician as any I've 'eard; and I've lived a long time listenin'," she said with some authority. "And aren't you a bright one to bring it today? Party in a box—that's what my late husband used to say of the accordion. Party in a box!

"Take a little sit-down now, ducky. They'll be along before you know it." She pulled a handful of knitting from her bag, sighed in happy anticipation, and settled back in her chair.

But I was too restless to sit. I stood at the edge of the rooftop and watched the crowds pour in—dense as molasses, filling every nook and cranny surrounding the station. It was mesmerizing. The sound that rose up was a peculiar mingling of thousands of voices—a low rumbling thunder set to burst.

And then, as if it were the keeper of time itself, the blue and silver train came steaming down the tracks to the very end of the line. Up rose the immense sound of tens of thousands of people cheering,

"The king is here! He is here!"

The twenty-one-gun boom of the royal salute came from the other side of the city. And with it, we, on the rooftop, joined our voices to the vastness of cheering people below.

Thunderous. Rapturous. Brilliant.

Magnifico! Oh, *magnifico!*

I lifted my hands and touched my earrings, feeling the smoothness, the luck Nonna had said I'd had with me since I was a baby—gifted with gold. The man who'd helped me up the stairs came near. He looked at my accordion and raised an eyebrow at me. I nodded, grand as a concertmaster giving a cue, and held out my arms.

Once the accordion was settled on my shoulders and I had my hands in place, I looked down to see the king solemnly step toward where the limousine and the queen were waiting. A few more hands to shake and they would be gone. Once more, I silently invoked Saint Cecilia and then...

"Bonnie Charlie's noo a-wa';

"Safely o'er the friendly main;

"Mony a heart will break in twa,

"Should he ne'er come back again."

At first I led only the voices on the rooftop—
and no more than a handful of people had ven-
tured up so high. But it caught in the air, as
quick as the blaze of a match, spreading down-
ward and into the crowd, igniting in everyone
the simple chorus:

"Will ye no come back again,

"Will ye no come back again?

"Better lo'ed ye canna be,

"Will ye no come back again?"

And the king turned slowly around, his face
upturned, his eyes searching the skyline, until
they met the spectacle on the rooftop of the
Ivanhoe. And he looked at me—right at me.

And he was pleased.

A reporter caught up to me afterward, when I
was nearly home.

"What could you see, so high up? From such a
great distance?" He sounded skeptical. He didn't
even take his notebook out.

I told him exactly what had happened. But I think he did not believe me. At least, there was never any story in the newspaper.

I told him I played the way my father told me to—proud, for all the neighbors to hear. I strained the bellows and squeezed as hard as I could, building to a bold crescendo and drawing out every ounce of volume the Camroni held inside. When the song was at its fullest, I saw his Majesty's black shoes, polished smooth as a mirror, gleaming in the morning sun. When I launched into the last verse, and the king raised one foot to lightly, regally, tap out the tune, in perfect time with me, we stayed there at the peak of the mountain, all the way through to the very last refrain.

That's what I wanted to remember forever.

And I have.

Afterword

"Often we spoke of the children of Canada, who thronged the cities and crowded the platforms at the little wayside stations that cheered us on our journey."

—*Queen Elizabeth, the Queen Mother*
(1900–2002), Ottawa, 1954

STRATHCONA IS one of Vancouver, British Columbia's oldest neighborhoods. At the time of this story, Lord Strathcona Elementary was known as the "school of many nationalities, but only one flag." Mr. Stefani's store was inspired by the Giuriato Brothers' grocery store in Strathcona. There was an "agony aunt," who gave advice to the lovelorn and who went by the pen name Dorothy Dix. An American, her real name was

Elizabeth Meriwether Gilmer, and from 1901 to 1951, her column ran in almost 300 newspapers in Canada and the United States.

Deepest gratitude for everyone who contributed major and minor chords to this story. Special thanks to Daniella Zamprogno and her parents, Augusta and Nerone Zamprogno, for the Italian (any errors in translation are solely my own) and for "Showen Tell." Thanks to Mike Pennock and the Fernie Museum and Historical Society; Christine Adams of www.accordions.com, Ivan Sayers for sharing his Eaton's catalogs from 1939; Joe Morelli, Al Denoni, and Karl Hergt for the accordion memories; Bessie Wapp for the lessons; Maureen Molloy for the saint suggestions; and Dr. Sharon Duncan for "saving" the thumb and two fingers of Gioseff's left hand.

To Ines Capon-Lomas, for remembering life in Strathcona in the thirties, and for being such a pleasure to talk to, my many thanks. And to my father, Larry Candido, who remembered wine in

Pepsi bottles and the story of Grandpa Marino Candido's only year in the Canadian school system (a bright ninth grader back in Italy, Marino was enrolled in the third grade in Canada at the age of fourteen because he couldn't speak English. After a year of frustration and humiliation, he quit but went on to learn perfect English, which he spoke with scarcely any trace of an accent).

That this story is now a book I am forever grateful to my agent, Elizabeth Harding, for her early enthusiasm and sustained confidence, Gail Winskill for embracing the manuscript, and Ann Featherstone for making it all better. And to Nicole Thibault, Janice Benedetti, and Jacqui Noftall, thank you.

Accordions have a history of being played at royal visits. According to **www.accordions.com**, accordion music was played in New Zealand for the 1901 visit of the Duke and Duchess of Cornwall, and also at the 1920 visit of the Prince of Wales.

It's believed that the first piano accordion appeared in Canada around 1930 and was brought to the country by Italian immigrants. "There are probably more accordions in closets than any other instrument in North America today," says veteran accordion teacher Al Denoni. Popular with parents, who foisted them upon their children, accordions in the earlier part of the twentieth century were a more affordable, and portable, alternative to the piano. In the 1930s, hundreds of kids made their way every week through the doors of Paramount Studios in Vancouver for accordion lessons. But by the time the Beatles appeared on "The Ed Sullivan Show" in 1964, the guitar was all the rage. The accordion was shunted into basements, attics, and closets. Today, if you dig around, you might find a "Black Maria," a Scandalli, a Camroni, or perhaps even a Hohner waiting patiently in your garage.

I did.